SPECIAL MESSAGE TO READERS

THE ULVERSCROFT FOUNDATION (registered UK charity number 264873) was established in 1972 to provide funds for research, diagnosis and treatment of eye diseases. Examples of major projects funded by the Ulverscroft Foundation are:

- The Children's Eye Unit at Moorfields Eye Hospital, London
- The Ulverscroft Children's Eye Unit at Great Ormond Street Hospital for Sick Children
- Funding research into eye diseases and treatment at the Department of Ophthalmology, University of Leicester
- The Ulverscroft Vision Research Group, Institute of Child Health
- Twin operating theatres at the Western Ophthalmic Hospital, London
- The Chair of Ophthalmology at the Royal Australian College of Ophthalmologists

You can help further the work of the Foundation by making a donation or leaving a legacy. Every contribution is gratefully received. If you would like to help support the Foundation or require further information, please contact:

THE ULVERSCROFT FOUNDATION
The Green, Bradgate Road, Anstey
Leicester LE7 7FU, England
Tel: (0116) 236 4325
website: www.ulverscroft-foundation.org.uk

OUT OF THE SHADOWS

1955. Clarissa finds herself having to deal with everyone else's problems at the expense of her own. Her mother's premature death has burdened her with the responsibility of running her parents' house at the expense of her artistic ambitions, while others around her seem to be enjoying the freedom she secretly craves. But then she meets Michael — and a world of possibilities opens up before her . . .

JOHN DARLEY

OUT OF THE SHADOWS

Complete and Unabridged

LINFORD
Leicester

First published in Great Britain in 2021

First Linford Edition
published 2022

Copyright © 2021 by DC Thomson & Co. Ltd.,
and John Darley
All rights reserved

*A catalogue record for this book is available
from the British Library.*

ISBN 978–1–4448–4972–1

Published by
Ulverscroft Limited
Anstey, Leicestershire

Printed and bound in Great Britain by
TJ Books Ltd., Padstow, Cornwall

This book is printed on acid-free paper

Keeping Up Appearances

Tennyson Avenue was in one of the most desirable areas of Chepswell.

Its line of elm trees on both sides of the pavement and the mixed hedging and shrubs of the front gardens gave it a distinct air of quiet, smug, undisturbed indifference to everywhere other than its own immediate, upper-middle-class environment.

Being far enough away from London had enabled it to avoid most of the German Luftwaffe's attempt at bringing the United Kingdom to its knees.

Only one bomb had landed within its municipal boundaries and that had been from a V1 which exploded slap-bang in the middle of Leyton Park.

The resulting damage had remained as a crater for a number of years after the war had ended, providing much-needed entertainment and exercise for boys on bikes and scooters.

Then, just last year, after a number of

complaints from the public that all these young 'hooligans' were lowering the tone of the neighbourhood, the borough council filled it in.

They restored the park to its previous condition, removing any sign of the crater ever having been there at all.

It was this sort of thing that helped the residents of the many suburban villas in this year of 1955 to be able to erase the small matter of a world war from their consciousness.

By doing so, they could continue with their lives as if nothing had ever happened to have disturbed their own insular tranquillity.

Clarissa Symons ('It's pronounced Simmons,' her mother, Dorothy, was for ever telling people) lived at number 48 The Cedars and hated every square inch of it.

At the age of eighteen and a half she had hoped that the end of the war might have brought a change of attitude and outlook amongst the residents round here.

However, just as with the filling-in of the bomb crater in Leyton Park, every hope that Clarissa may have held for change had been buried.

She had ambitions to be an artist but both her parents considered it a waste of time and education.

'Surely you can come up with something better than that?' Dorothy Symons scolded her.

Clarissa could almost hear the addition to this sentence which, if not on her mother's lips, was certainly in her mind.

'What would the neighbours think?'

Living under this stifling, restrictive control, where your behaviour and appearance was dictated as much for the benefit of your neighbours as it was for one's parents, was making Clarissa harbour a rebellious resentment.

It was a resentment which, though at present dormant, would inevitably bring about changes that no-one could have foreseen.

It wouldn't be the Easter Holiday fair that would cause it, although that would be the catalyst for change . . .

'Of course you cannot go to the fair, Clarissa.'

There it was again, that unspoken sentence, hovering in the air above mother and daughter.

'What would the neighbours think?'

'But it's OK for Terry to go?'

Clarissa saw Mrs Symons freeze as she tried to control the paroxysm of rage which her daughter's use of the word 'OK' had aroused.

Clarissa had deliberately used the slang term, knowing full well that her mother would be appalled.

In Mrs Symons's imagination 'OK' would conjure up images of gum-chewing Teddy boys and totally unsuitable jazz music.

'Where on earth did you learn to use that awful expression, Clarissa? As for your brother, he's not only older than you but he is also much more responsible.

'Surely you wouldn't begrudge Terry a little harmless pleasure whilst he's home on leave! Besides, he will be taking Eleanor and they certainly won't want you tagging along.'

Clarissa despaired of trying to reason with her mother. Of course she wouldn't begrudge her brother his enjoyment.

Terry was partway through his National Service and this was the first break he would be having for some time.

He would be keen to spend time with his fiancée as well as his family.

As for her father, to Clarissa he just seemed some sort of shadowy figure who only held views on business and commerce, allowing his wife to be in charge of all matters domestic.

It was so frustrating!

At least she had an ally in her friend. Lorraine Cutler — on the surface, at least — was everything that Clarissa's mother could wish for in a daughter.

Had she known the truth about this young Sunday school teacher she might have felt differently.

Like Clarissa, Lorraine felt stifled by the values that many parents, including their own, held on to so stubbornly. The war had done nothing to change this older generation's minds.

There was none of that 'live today, for tomorrow we may die' attitude with them. It was more like 'let's continue living for yesterday in the hope that those outdated values might somehow return'.

★ ★ ★

'I'm telling you, Lorrie, I'm just about up to here with Mother's constant criticism,' Clarissa told her friend as they walked together to school on a warm and sunny April morning.

'You don't have to tell me,' Lorraine replied. 'My mother's much the same. 'Don't do this, don't do that'.'

The two friends continued on their way, exchanging anecdotes of each other's latest injustice.

Though similar in interests and attitudes, the girls were almost extreme opposites in appearance.

Clarissa was of a fair complexion with

very striking blue eyes. Her hair, straight and also fair, was usually tied back in a ponytail. She was an inch or so taller than Lorraine and slimmer.

Lorraine had short, wavy, brown hair which seemed to have no direction or style yet fitted around her pretty face in a flattering way.

Her eyes were brown and wider than Clarissa's, giving the impression that she was in a constant state of mild surprise.

Her uniform didn't so much fit her as she fitted into it. Clarissa, on the other hand, looked elegant and graceful despite the school uniform.

Even the way she carried her satchel gave it more the impression of a chic handbag than being simply a holder for her school books.

'Are you going to the fair?' Lorraine asked after they'd finally finished discussing the trials of being daughters of unsympathetic parents.

'Mother said no but, yes, I will be going.'

'Your brother's bound to go. What if

he sees you? Won't he tell?'

For all their similar age, Lorraine would often refer to things in an almost childlike manner, as now, for instance.

It rankled Clarissa ever so slightly that her friend should be throwing up obstacles in her path.

It was almost as if she didn't want Clarissa to go.

She was also slightly puzzled that Lorraine clearly already knew that Terry was going to be at home for that upcoming weekend, but she decided to let it pass.

'I really don't care. All I know is I'm going, and nothing's going to stop me!'

Fortune Smiles

Saying you're going to do something is quite often a lot easier than actually doing it, as Clarissa was beginning to find out.

Her mother seemed to be keeping an even closer eye on her than usual, constantly busying her with chores around the house that would normally be the domain of Mrs Gibbs, the daily.

This in itself was a source of irritation to the young girl — this assumption that a girl's place and purpose was set firmly within the confines of a family home, with all its attendant drudgery.

Clarissa pictured a world beyond this suburban avenue of trees. One day, she knew, she would find it.

But again the question arose as to how this could be achieved.

The fair duly arrived in Chepswell, in Leyton Park. Clarissa and Lorraine would manage, by convoluted means, to pass by it on a daily basis, watching the progress of its construction on the larger of the park's two fields.

It was to be up and running over the Easter school holiday and it was astonishing — and exciting — to see the progress being made each time the two girls passed.

'Look, Clarry, they've got the dodgems set up!' Lorraine cried excitedly. 'I love the dodgems. I will definitely be going on them.'

'Me, too,' Clarissa said, but with less conviction than her friend.

She still hadn't worked out a plan to make it possible for her to go. It was a bit of a mystery how Lorraine hadn't encountered any objections from her parents, especially as they were friends with Clarissa's, with their weekly bridge meetings alternating at each other's houses.

Perhaps it had something to do with Lorraine being a Sunday school teacher — that assumption that she would never 'stray from the path of goodness'.

Clarissa had stopped going to church some years ago. It was not that she didn't believe — she did — but her faith belonged outside in the real world.

That was where God was much more evident than in the stuffy, dark, enclosed space of the church which her mother still attended.

★ ★ ★

The start of the school holidays arrived and, with it, Terry on his brief leave from the Army.

Clarissa, although pleased to see her brother, had to conceal the resentment she felt at the treatment he received on his return home. The prodigal son came to mind.

Nevertheless, it was good to see him and he seemed to have brought good weather with him, too, sunny and warm, which was perfect for whatever leisure plans anyone might have.

Clarissa still hadn't come up with a plan for going to the fair and she was getting desperate.

One thing that did happen, and which presented her with an opportunity for achieving her aim, was provided by Terry's fiancée, Eleanor Tompkins.

Eleanor had telephoned to say she wasn't feeling well and would be staying at home for the immediate future. This would put Terry at a loose end.

The journey to Eleanor's house was quite long, requiring two bus changes. The Sunday service which would be in operation over the whole coming weekend didn't inspire Terry to make the effort to go and visit the invalid.

He actually had a motorbike but it wasn't working as it needed new spark plugs. Clarissa wasn't sure her parents knew about the bike. Surely they wouldn't approve.

'I'll just have to go to the fair by myself,' he said to no-one in particular.

Clarissa sensed a slight hint of relief in his voice as he spoke. Things hadn't been going too well between Terry and Eleanor, almost from the day when their engagement had been announced in the 'Chepswell Gazette'.

Clarissa got the impression that Terry felt under pressure to settle down. Despite being nearly two years older than Clarissa, her brother often seemed less mature than she was.

He worked in a bank and had met Eleanor one lunch hour in Littlewoods' restaurant. Standing in front of him in the queue, she discovered she did not have enough money to pay for her lunch.

To save her embarrassment — and because she was very pretty — Terry had stepped in and made up the difference. From there they had shared a table to eat their lunch and things developed.

Somehow, Mrs Symons had managed to propel the romance between the young couple at a far faster pace than Terry had intended.

He still had many things he wanted to do, plus there was that dark, ominous cloud in the form of National Service constantly hanging over him at the time.

However, even this prospect Mrs Symons managed to turn to advantage.

'It would be a comfort both to me and Eleanor if there was a definite commitment between you both, when and wherever you may be during your time serving your country.'

It had worked, a bit like a magic trick. Terry and Eleanor had announced their engagement at a special party organised by both mothers at the Freemasons Hall.

Clarissa had gone to great lengths both to please her parents and the engaged couple by dressing up for the occasion and being amicable to all parties.

However, as far as Eleanor was concerned, it wasn't working. Neither girl would be able to explain why, but there was no rapport between them.

'I do like your dress,' Clarissa had said to Eleanor.

'Thanks,' Eleanor had replied.

And that was how it continued — Clarissa trying to open a conversation and Eleanor shutting each attempt down with monosyllabic responses.

As to the present situation, Clarissa had an idea. If Terry was now going to the fair on his own, surely it would be perfectly reasonable for Clarissa to accompany him.

'Fine by me,' he said when she begged her brother to let her come along.

'Will you ask Mother? Only, I know if I do she'll say no.'

'OK.' Terry smiled, sharing their joke of using inappropriate expressions which both knew their mother would have loathed.

Surprisingly, Mrs Symons raised no objections when Terry put the proposal to her.

She had been feeling below par for a few days now, although any suggestion of calling Dr Anderson she swiftly rejected.

'It's nothing, just a touch of heartburn,' she assured everyone, which sufficed for her husband and son.

Clarissa, however, had misgivings and wondered if she ought to stay with her and not go to the fair.

'Don't be silly, dear, you go and enjoy

yourself,' her mother said from the armchair in the sitting-room.

As Clarissa got up to leave, Mrs Symons reached out and took her daughter's arm.

'I do want you to enjoy yourself, you know. Truly I do.'

These words were to haunt Clarissa for a long time to come.

The Fun of the Fair

The Saturday of the fair's opening arrived and the weather continued to embrace Chepswell with clear blue skies and warm sunshine.

Mrs Symons's condition still had not shown any signs of improving but, as Terry pointed out, it wasn't any worse.

'What time will we be going?' Clarissa asked her brother.

'Not too early. I think these places always look at their best when it's dark and all the lights are on. Gives it a magic quality.'

Clarissa nodded, smiling.

It was true, there was something both exciting and dangerous — in the romantic sense — of a fairground at night. The lights, together with the swirling music, laughter and screams made the perfect ingredients for such a venue.

She could hardly wait. She accepted that it was an almost childish feeling she was experiencing but she couldn't help it.

Maybe, tonight, something wonderfully unexpected might happen.

For some reason, as she thought this, the expression 'Be careful what you wish for' ran through her head.

Finally it was time to set off. The sun was still some way off from setting but the heat of the day was already beginning to cool.

Mrs Symons managed to refrain from disapproving of her daughter's choice of outfit. Clarissa had opted for navy trousers and a maroon jumper.

Terry wore a jumper, too, plus his old, baggy, corduroy trousers.

'I bet we look a right pair walking down Tennyson Avenue. The curtains will be twitching from every window.'

Suddenly, Terry took his sister's arm and they set off, singing 'We're A Couple Of Swells'. They ended up laughing too much to continue.

Clarissa was enjoying Terry's company, something she'd not had the benefit of since he'd started going out with Eleanor.

A thought occurred to her.

'Did Eleanor's father ask you what your intentions were towards his daughter?'

Terry grinned.

'Stop it, now. Eleanor's family's not like that. Obviously, they want the best for their daughter, same as Mum and Dad want for you. It's only natural.'

'You sound as Victorian as they do,' Clarissa countered. 'Is my only purpose in life to be a good wife to someone? I tell you now, I have other plans.'

Terry stopped and turned Clarissa to face him. He shook his head but looked proud.

'I hope they happen for you, I really do.'

She slipped her arm through his and they continued on their way.

★ ★ ★

The bright, colourful lights were beginning to show more vividly as the sun slipped down behind the distant Chepswell hills.

The fair was busy and crowded; people were already queueing to go on the various rides. Some families were making their way out of the fairground, fathers carrying either tired offspring or coveted prizes.

For Clarissa the night was just beginning. The sounds, sights and scents all combined to give her a feeling of anticipation.

The fair brought something of the child out in her and clearly it was having a similar impact on her brother.

He'd already won Clarissa a prize on the firing range, having knocked three battered tin ducks down in rapid succession.

'Choose your prize, Clarrie,' he said as he passed the air rifle back to the showman.

Clarissa shrugged.

'What would Eleanor like, do you think?'

Terry didn't reply immediately and

over his face flashed an expression of exasperation. He quickly recovered, regaining his smile.

'Eleanor doesn't care for these sort of things.' He gestured towards the fluffy animals which were on display. 'Choose whatever you like.'

In the end, Clarissa opted for a small, pink rabbit. She would have preferred one of the larger teddies but two things prevented her.

Firstly, she might get tired from carrying it around, which would hamper her enjoyment. Secondly, her mother would be appalled by the sight of something so 'frightfully vulgar'.

Even though the picture of her saying this was clear and vivid in Clarissa's mind, she also knew a sense of guilt and misgiving as she thought this.

She shivered.

'Are you cold?'

She turned towards her brother. He was smiling at her and it was enough to dispel that feeling of apprehension which had overwhelmed her seconds before.

'No, I'm fine. Thanks for Bunny.'

Terry looked around him.

'Listen, would you mind if we split up for a while? I've just seen some of my pals and I wouldn't mind a chance to catch up with them. Is that OK?'

'Of course, Terry. I'm hoping to meet up with Lorraine, anyway. You go.'

'Lorraine?' Terry's expression suddenly changed as if a light had been switched on. 'Do you think she'll be here?'

She'd not seen that look of hopeful expectation on his face for some time — probably not since he and Eleanor had got engaged.

'She said she would. Why?'

Ignoring her question, he looked at his watch.

'We'll meet up at ten over where we came in. See you.'

And with that he was gone, more hurriedly than there seemed any reason to be.

Clarissa did her best to hide her disappointment.

She wished that Terry hadn't decided to go off. But, of course, why wouldn't he?

He could hardly be expected to chaperone his sister, who was perfectly capable of taking care of herself.

Even so, the haste at which he had departed puzzled Clarissa.

A New Acquaintance

'That's a cute bunny. Has it got a name?'

Clarissa turned to the voice and found herself looking into the clear blue eyes of the most good-looking boy she had ever seen, even in this light.

She ordered herself to be careful, not let her attraction show. At the same time, it would seem rude not to respond.

One of the many things that her mother had taught her was that there was never any excuse for being rude and inconsiderate.

'I haven't thought of one yet,' she mumbled.

The young man considered.

'Well, as it's pink I don't think Thumper would be appropriate. My name's Michael, by the way.'

He held out his hand for Clarissa to shake, which she did. As well as being extremely good looking he also, it seemed, had impeccable manners.

'I'm Clarissa, Clarissa Symons.'

'Really?' Michael smiled, looking surprised. 'I've heard my sister mention you. I believe you're in her class. Aileen Parkes. Do you know her?'

Clarissa did, but only through her name being called out on the register.

Aileen was one of those girls you only ever saw the back of, as she would invariably be seated up front in the school room. She was zealous when it came to education.

Having got the introductions over with, Michael made a suggestion.

'I'd like to have a go on the dodgems but it seems rather pointless to try to have fun on your own. Perhaps you'd care to join me?'

With no sign of Lorraine, who was obviously not coming despite all she'd said, Clarissa could think of no reason to refuse.

The two of them joined the waiting throng and were soon sharing a car together.

'Shall I drive or would you prefer to?' Michael asked.

In other circumstances Clarissa might have insisted on taking the wheel as an indication of her determination not to be undermined or patronised by the male of the species.

Michael's old-fashioned politeness and charm seemed to please her and persuade her to think otherwise for once.

'No, you drive. I'm fine.'

They had two goes, for which Michael insisted on paying each time. Then they tried the traditional carousel with its rising and falling horses. That was fun, too.

Time flew by. They told each other about themselves and she learned Michael worked at the Clevedale Hotel.

Clarissa noticed just in time that it was very nearly 10 o'clock.

'I must go. Thank you for a lovely time.'

'May I see you home?' Michael asked.

Clarissa hesitated, then she shook her head.

'No, thank you.'

'Well, can I see you again?'

Again she hesitated. He was a really

nice, good-looking boy, but what was the point? There could be no future in their forming a relationship.

Clarissa had bigger, broader plans for her life and she did not want them to be compromised by a romantic entanglement.

'I expect we'll see each other around,' she said finally. 'Now I must go. Bye.'

She made her way towards the entrance where Terry had said he would meet her.

There were a lot more people at the fair than when she and her brother had arrived, and with it being dark Clarissa found herself disoriented and unsure which way to go.

As she turned down a particularly dimly lit pathway between some of the stalls she could see, ahead of her, two people.

It was a boy and a girl, their arms linked together as they kissed passionately.

There was something vaguely familiar about them both, something which became shockingly apparent as they drew apart.

Yet still Clarissa could not believe it. Terry, her brother, with Lorraine, her best friend?

* * *

Clarissa turned back and ran from this bewildering scene. As she did, a figure leaped back into the shadowed concealment between two stalls.

Michael could just make out Clarissa's features and was aware of the look of distress on her face.

A moment later a voice called out to her; a man was running towards her. Once he'd caught up with her he muttered something which Michael could not hear, then put his arm around her shoulder, accompanying her out of the fairground.

'No wonder she didn't want to see me again,' Michael whispered to himself bitterly. 'She's already got a boyfriend.'

He came out from the shadows, took a deep breath and turned to go back into the fair.

The expression 'Plenty more fish' nagged at him, but it offered no comfort.

Emergency

Neither Terry nor Clarissa made mention of what had just occurred; instead, they exchanged stilted pleasantries about their experience of tonight's fair.

Clarissa was still in shock, having witnessed the passionate embrace between her brother and Lorraine.

It was not so much the betrayal of Terry towards his fiancée, it was more the sight of Lorraine behaving like a femme fatale — Lorraine, the Sunday school teacher.

It was like something straight out of the pages of the 'News Of The World'.

Further, unwished-for thoughts on the matter were suddenly interrupted as home came into view. Outside their house, alarmingly, was parked an ambulance.

Clarissa and Terry stopped in their tracks.

'What's that doing there?'

Terry didn't wait to find out. He

sprinted off, leaving Clarissa frozen in fear on the pavement.

She quickly recovered, however, and also ran towards the house. She was still some way off as two ambulance men appeared, holding a stretcher at each end.

Lying on it, covered only by a grey hospital blanket, was Dorothy Symons. Even from the distance that still separated Clarissa from her mother she could see how pale and surprisingly small she looked.

'Mother!' Clarissa waved, knowing as she did so what a totally futile and inappropriate action it was.

On either side of Mrs Symons were her husband, Geoffrey, and Terry. Behind this sombre procession came the slightly stooped figure of Dr Anderson, whose hand gripped his distinctive black bag.

It was a frightening tableau.

'What's happened? Mother!' Clarissa called out as the ambulance men put Mrs Symons into the ambulance. 'Mother!'

Terry took hold of his sister.

'Dad found her on the sitting-room floor. She was barely conscious.'

Mr Symons, looking ashen, barely acknowleged the presence of his daughter. He climbed into the back of the ambulance, leaving his children standing in the road.

'Which hospital are you taking her to?' Clarissa asked the driver as he was about to get into his cab.

'The Infirmary, love. Up on Spiersley Street.'

Clarissa turned to her brother.

'We must go.'

'I'll get my motorbike,' Terry called as he sped off to the garage.

Clarissa, waiting, could not believe what had happened.

The avenue gave nothing away; all was still and quiet as it invariably was every evening of every day.

But nothing was still and quiet inside Clarissa. She felt an overwhelming anxiousness — almost panic — totally out of keeping with the setting.

She heard Terry's motorbike rev up

and seconds later he appeared out of the gravelled driveway.

A fleeting thought ran through her mind as he approached. What had happened to make his motorbike suddenly work again when, at the time he'd decided he couldn't go and see Eleanor during her illness, he'd said it needed new plugs?

'Jump on and hold tight!' he shouted.

Clarissa did as he told her and then the machine roared off, waking up the inhabitants of the avenue where nothing ever happened.

In the gutter, near where the ambulance had been parked, lay a hastily abandoned pink rabbit.

Your Fault

'She's had a slight stroke,' Geoffrey Symons told his children when they eventually found him in the maze of corridors of St Bartholemew's, known locally as St Barts. 'That's what they think.'

Their father had never been one for showing any physical affection and it was difficult for Clarissa, at least, to offer any support or comfort other than by words.

'I'm sure she'll be fine,' she told him, trying to convince herself at the same time. 'She's in the right place.'

'Can we see her?' Terry asked.

Mr Symons shook his head.

'Not at the moment. They're carrying out tests, trying to establish the extent of . . .'

He couldn't finish saying what he knew was going on — that they were trying to establish what damage her stroke might have caused, permanent or otherwise.

Again, Clarissa could offer only words as solace. This man was almost a stranger.

Most days he would be gone to the office before she was up, and in the evenings he seemed to hide behind his newspaper, as if it could shield him from his family.

Terry went off to see what more he could find out. Clarissa, noticing some chairs against the wall behind them, suggested to her father that he might want to sit down.

Instead of doing so, he turned to face his daughter, an expression of hostility set into his ashen features.

'This is all your fault!' he said with such vindictiveness that Clarissa felt as if she'd been shot.

She had to reach out for the wall behind her to stop herself from falling down.

'If you hadn't gone to the fair this would never have happened!'

Recovering slightly from the shock of what her father had just said, she tried to defend herself.

'Mother was quite happy for me to go, and Terry. I went with him, remember!'

'Don't bring Terry into this. You're her daughter; you should have known better!'

Clarissa did not know how to respond and decided to say nothing. She preferred to think that her father was suffering from shock and that he didn't know what he was saying.

Terry returned, unaware of what had just taken place. He no doubt imagined that the expressions on his sister's and father's face were to do with Mrs Symons's condition.

'I found a doctor,' he told them. 'He didn't know anything but said he'd find out for us. So all we can do is wait.'

He looked around him.

'I wonder if there's anywhere where we could get a cup of tea.'

A nurse, young and attractive, was coming along the corridor. Terry stepped out in front of her, smiling broadly.

'Excuse me, is there a canteen anywhere round here? We'd like to get a cup of tea.'

The nurse checked the watch pinned

to her uniform.

'I'm afraid they're closed now,' she said, smiling back. 'I do have a flask of coffee; you're welcome to share it with me.'

'Oh, I couldn't possibly do that,' Terry said, without meaning it.

'Please do; I never drink it all anyway. I'm due a break, so if you'd care to follow me I'll find a cup and you can have some.'

'Thank you so much.'

Terry walked off with the young nurse, not once turning to look back and see the expression of disbelief on Clarissa's face.

Mr Symons had now sat down and was staring into space. Clarissa sat in a chair a couple of spaces away from her father.

She still felt incredibly hurt by what he had said.

'How could it possibly be my fault?' she asked herself. 'Mother was happy enough for me to go. Besides, there was no sign of her becoming this unwell.'

So the time passed. Clarissa's brother eventually returned, looking very pleased with himself.

'How was your coffee?' Clarissa asked with more than a hint of sarcasm.

'Fine,' he said. 'Just what I needed. Any news?'

Mr Symons looked up at his son and shook his head.

★ ★ ★

Dawn was just beginning to break when, finally, a doctor approached, accompanied by a nurse.

Nothing in their poker faces gave any indication of what they knew and what the doctor was about to impart.

'Mr Symons?'

The doctor directed his gaze at Geoffrey Symons, who, sensing bad news, slowly got to his feet.

Clarissa, also apprehensive, tried to take her father's arm but he shook it off, never moving his eyes from the doctor's.

'I'm sorry, Mr Symons. Your wife died

a few minutes ago.

'I'm afraid there was an embolism which cut off the blood to her brain, which then caused her heart to arrest. There was nothing we could do.'

His face slackened a little and there was genuine compassion in his eyes.

'I truly am sorry for your loss. I'll leave you with Nurse Robbins. Good morning.'

Then, in his more accustomed professional manner, the doctor walked away down the corridor, leaving Nurse Robbins to deal with the aftermath of this most devastating news.

'We have a room for relatives if you'd care to sit there for a while until we're ready.'

'Ready?' Terry echoed. 'Ready for what?'

Clarissa shot her brother a glance, appalled at his apparent flippancy.

But then she could see, from the look and colour — or lack of it — on his face, that he was as devastated as she was.

Nurse Robbins didn't act surprised.

'I imagine you would like to see Mrs Symons. We just need a few minutes to prepare her.'

Clarissa could not imagine what there was to prepare. Her mother, after all, would still be dead.

How was it, she wondered, that the end of someone's life could be just the start of problems for those left behind.

Already Clarissa, despite herself, was starting to fear the consequences that this tragedy was going to bring to her.

She turned slightly to look at her father. He seemed not to be fully aware of what had happened, of what he had lost.

But, then, she reasoned, if unfairly, it was not as likely in the long term to impact on his life as it would do on Clarissa's.

This was still only 1955, after all. Women and girls were not generally expected to have many or indeed any ambitions beyond home and marriage.

This state of affairs was suffocating, especially for a keenly intelligent, ambitious girl like Clarissa.

She tried to stop having these selfish thoughts in the midst of all this. But, deep down, she was harbouring an unreasonable resentment for what had happened to her mother.

'Why did you have to die?' she was thinking. 'Why, oh, why?'

'Sis? Are you all right?'

Of course she wasn't. And she wondered if ever she'd be all right again.

At the Graveside

More than three months on from Mrs Symons's death nothing had changed, yet everything had changed.

Clarissa often had such thoughts, especially when, as now, she was at her mother's grave, changing the flowers.

She gave the unnecessarily elaborate headstone a cursory wipe. Although the choice of headstone had been her father's, Clarissa had to concede how suitable her mother would have felt it was.

Even in death there clung on this need to keep up appearances.

She continued kneeling in front of the grave, recalling how she had found herself in this situation today.

She had imagined she would have been at art college by now, but her father wouldn't hear of it.

'Art is a hobby, not a career, especially for a girl. No, I shall need you at home now. I've already dismissed Mrs Gibbs, so there's an end of it!'

As Clarissa walked away from the grave and out of the churchyard which contained it she noticed a figure, familiar yet remote, watching her.

It was Michael Parkes, she realised — elder brother of Aileen, the school swot.

Clarissa almost used to feel sorry for Aileen, who seemed to have no life other than what the school provided for her.

How ironic it was that here was Clarissa, the one with all the big ideas and ambitions, stuck at home housekeeping.

By contrast, Aileen had been offered a place at Oxford University, no less, and from what Clarissa had heard had come right out of her shell.

Clarissa kept her eyes focused on the ground as she headed for the lych gate, but even so it was no surprise when she came face to face with Michael inside its roofed space.

He was looking very smart — and very handsome — in his RAF uniform.

'Hello, Clarissa. How are you?'

There was still that charming, yet

outdated, gentlemanly way with him. Today, however, it actually irritated Clarissa as it seemed patronising, even while she realised she was probably being unfair to him.

'I'm fine, thanks. I've just been seeing to my mother's grave.'

'Of course.'

His voice fell away, seeming unsure how to reference the obvious fact that Mrs Symons was dead, despite the close proximity of her grave.

For someone of a similar age to Clarissa's brother he carried off a much more mature aspect than Terry probably ever would, she felt.

The silence between them grew longer. At last she steered the subject away from her own circumstances.

Clarissa was tired of the subject of her mother's death, and of her own purpose in life and topic of conversation being seemingly centred around it.

'How are you? I take it that you're no longer working up at the Clevedale Hotel?'

'No, as you can see I'm doing my National Service. I've just finished my basic training at Duxford and now I'm waiting to see where I'll get posted.

'Fortunately I managed to finish my training at the hotel so I am now a fully qualified chef.'

Clarissa nodded. Her brother was still doing his, in the Army, and, by all accounts was enjoying every minute of it, despite still being engaged to Eleanor.

Terry had probably been glad to get back amongst the living, away from the depressing atmosphere that now permeated number 48 The Cedars.

Nothing had changed with regard to Terry's engagement to Eleanor but, apart from the occasion of Mrs Symons's funeral, the young couple had not been together since.

Clarissa could not understand why her brother was continuing with the charade, although she had never made known to him what she had seen between him and her best friend, Lorraine.

'Well,' she said now as another, more

awkward silence descended. 'I'd best be getting back; housework to do, meals to prepare. Nice to see you.'

She started to walk past Michael but he, very gently, took her arm to halt her.

She couldn't know it had been some time before he had learned that the boy Clarissa had been with at the fair that night was, in fact, her brother, Terry.

He had felt a fool for not realising it sooner; they had got on so well during the brief time they were together at the fair.

Now it seemed that everything was back as before he'd spoken to her for that first time.

'I'd very much like to see you again, Clarissa. How about going to the cinema one evening? Or maybe a walk, perhaps.'

Clarissa was both flattered and puzzled. Obviously her circumstances since her mother's untimely death had changed. But why was he asking her now?

Why, when Clarissa was so weighed down with domestic drudgery and still trying to come to terms with her mother's untimely death, had Michael now appeared on the scene?

'I don't think so,' she said without looking him in the eye. 'I don't have a lot of free time; things are always so busy at home.'

Michael was not to be fobbed off so easily.

'Listen, Clarissa. If it's me you don't like, that's fine, I'll leave you alone.

'It's just that we seemed to be getting on so well at the fair, and then . . .'

'And then my mother died!'

The harsh words fell between them.

There was nothing Michael could say in response; anything he might come up with could sound heartless and selfish.

'I have to go,' Clarissa finally said, brushing past him.

A Garden Refuge

Clarissa was in the large garden of her parents' property. It was made up of formal beds and borders plus one or two ornamental trees. There was a herbaceous border set against a south-facing wall.

A great number of its plants, encouraged by the continuing warm summer weather, were out, providing a spectacle of mixed colours and tones from the diminutive dwarf pink campanulas fringing the front edge to the bold kniphofias and delphiniums.

These last stood close to the garden wall where clematis and virginia creeper gave contrast to this summer show. Their appearance in the July sunshine made Clarissa feel more cheerful — certainly more cheerful than she had felt this morning when speaking to Michael.

She was sitting on the lawn alongside the vegetable plot that she had dug and planted. It had become an immense source of pride and comfort to her, especially now, when she was able to look at the results of her efforts.

She could see that there were green beans to be picked, plus some more of her new potatoes to dig up. There was a neverending supply of tomatoes, those for salads and the Tom Thumb variety for making chutney.

This had been one of the few positives coming from her mother's death — she had discovered she had a true affinity with the earth.

In many ways it was as creative as anything she had done in art. Not just with the vegetables and salads she was growing but also with the flowers she'd sown.

There were already enough of the more traditional blooms in the garden, from early crocus and cyclamen through to daffodils, tulips and then the roses, of course.

These were all very welcome when they made their initial appearances, but Clarissa's creative side wanted to discover and produce more.

She saw it very much like painting — you mixed your colours on a palette and made a pleasing picture from them all.

It still surprised her that she continued to gain joy from being close to the earth, working in harmony with the seasons.

She knew she could never explain it to anyone; not to her father or even her brother.

Michael might understand, but she couldn't afford the risk. Her mother's death and this new, insular way of life had brought about vulnerability and fear in Clarissa.

She found it hard to trust or believe people; did they really mean what they said?

Did Michael really want to see her?

Her father's indifference towards her, seeing her as not much more than a servant; her brother's philanderings, despite remaining engaged to Eleanor . . . none of these things inspired confidence.

A thrush burst into song in the

ornamental cherry tree further down the garden.

Its sweet sound brought Clarissa out of her thoughts as she sat and listened to the mellifluous notes emanating from the bird.

'Someone's happy,' she whispered.

Even if the bird's purpose was merely to proclaim its territory, nevertheless it evoked a feeling in Clarissa which was the nearest to happiness that she had known for a very long time.

What a Mess

'Lorrie?' Clarissa, having opened the front door to persistent knocking, was surprised to see her friend, Lorraine, on the other side.

'Can I come in, Clarissa?'

Several alarm bells were ringing in Clarissa's head.

As 'Lorrie' was to 'Lorraine', so 'Clarry' was to 'Clarissa'. Why this new formality?

And why the urgent banging on the door?

Fortunately it was a working day; Geoffrey Symons was at the office, otherwise he would have been extremely annoyed by the disturbance.

Clarissa stepped aside for her friend to enter. They walked through the wide hallway into the sitting-room where Lorraine dropped on to the sofa, wringing her hands.

'Is something the matter?' Clarissa asked, already knowing there was.

'You could say that.'

She looked up at her friend, her eyes wide not with surprise but fear.

'Terry's not here, is he?'

'No, he's still doing his National Service. We're not expecting him home for another month or so.'

Clarissa came and sat down next to Lorraine and tried taking one of her hands, but there was no prising them apart.

'Would you like a cup of tea?'

As she offered she realised how ingrained domesticity had become in her life.

'I'd rather have something stronger, if you've got it!'

Clarissa turned to see what there was on her father's drinks tray on the sideboard. Whisky and brandy were both decanted.

That just left sherry and a half-full bottle of advocaat left over from Christmas.

Clarissa named them all but Lorraine shook her head.

'I don't want anything. Oh, Clarry!'

She leaned into her friend and began sobbing uncontrollably.

'Everything's a mess; it's all a mess!.'

Clarissa put an arm round her friend in an attempt to comfort her.

Although she had no idea what the 'mess' could be she had a suspicion that her brother was involved.

Since the time Clarissa had seen the two of them together at the fair, Terry had gone out on numerous occasions without saying where he was going or who he was seeing.

He was a grown man, of course, so he wasn't obliged to tell her his plans, but one person he definitely wasn't seeing on those evenings was Eleanor, his fiancée.

As Clarissa tried to soothe Lorraine a worrying phrase entered her head.

'Breach of promise'.

Such things were still being reported in the newspapers. The thought of it now caused Clarissa to shudder.

What would her mother have made of this? Or might Mrs Symons have better accepted the idea than Clarissa?

Still, it was hard to imagine — despite the evidence of her own eyes — that her brother and Lorraine could be so romantically involved with one another that they would risk bringing shame on their families.

'You asked if Terry was here, Lorrie. Why?'

She had to pull Lorraine's limp frame up into a sitting position so that she could see her response. Her friend's eyes were puffy with crying and there were shadows, too, as if she had not been getting sleep lately.

Lorraine took out a hanky and began drying her eyes. It seemed to Clarissa that she was buying time before she spoke.

When she did actually speak, Clarissa wasn't sure she had heard properly.

'Say that again!'

'Oh, don't make me, Clarry, it's hard enough admitting it to myself.'

'And Terry is the father?'

Lorraine nodded.

'He doesn't know, though. You're the

only one I've told. Clarry, what am I going to do?'

Well, you could pull yourself together, for a start, Clarissa thought, pushing her friend away from her.

This was too awful for tears. Too awful for anything in her limited experience of life.

Why was it, she thought, that the only people who seemed to come to her came with problems which they then tried to pass on?

She screamed inside, desperate to escape this whole, dreadful situation where it was certain that no happy ending was going to take place.

Nevertheless, she couldn't abandon her friend — her best friend.

Clarissa would have to try to help in some way, if only as a sort of mediator or go-between.

★ ★ ★

From that moment, any peace that the garden had to offer seemed hard to achieve, despite Clarissa often being out there to tend to her vegetable plot or deadhead the roses.

These were producing bloom after splendid bloom far beyond their season.

She could find no solace or long-term distraction from the seemingly insurmountable problems facing her brother, his fiancée and her friend.

She was suspecting that it was herself who was most troubled by it all. Once Lorraine had unburdened herself to Clarissa the problem seemed to become hers.

It was like pass the parcel, where everyone knew that the prize wasn't worth having and so they were trying to pass it on to the next person.

The trouble was, once it had reached Clarissa, there was no-one left to pass it to!

Her father could not be told.

'Not under any circumstances,' Terry ordered her once she'd informed him of Lorraine's 'situation'.

Now, to add to an already tangled

situation, Lorraine kept coming round to Clarissa's, sometimes on her way to school and always on her way home.

It struck Clarissa as unfair that she was being encumbered with so many people's problems, none of her making. She had enough to contend with in running this household.

'I need to get out of here,' she told herself, opening the telephone directory.

On the Heath

Michael was surprised by Clarissa's phone call, especially after she'd been so offhand with him outside the church.

But he wasn't going to dwell on that, nor let it affect him as he rummaged in his wardrobe looking for something appropriate to wear.

Clarissa had finally agreed to the walk he'd suggested at their earlier meeting. It was fortunate that he still had a couple of days of leave left.

Now there was just the matter of what might constitute walking apparel.

Michael did have a pair of sturdy walking boots and some old corduroy trousers, plus a well-worn Norfolk jacket. But, apart from the fact that it was a very warm day, it was not the attire with which he hoped to impress Clarissa.

In the end he stepped out of his house wearing a checked shirt with sleeves rolled up, plus a cravat. For trousers he'd decided to stick with the corduroy, hoping they lent a rural rather than a rustic quality.

Instead of boots he wore a favourite old pair of tan brogues.

Surprisingly, Clarissa was already coming down the garden path as Michael reached her drive.

'I'm not late, am I?'

'Not at all.'

Clarissa smiled, melting Michael's heart. She had not smiled at all when he'd spoken to her at the church. Now it was as if the sun had burst through a cloud, shining warmth and light on everything.

'I couldn't stay indoors a moment longer,' she told him as they set off together at a brisk pace in the opposite direction from which Michael had come.

He was trying to assess her appearance as they walked. Her clothes didn't give the impression of someone going on a hike, which made him feel he'd got his own outfit hideously wrong.

Clarissa wore a rather chic mauve beret which simply added to the sweet sophistication of her looks.

Beneath this was a pale pink, long-sleeved blouse. Instead of trousers, which were still quite frowned upon in this upper-middle-class neighbourhood, Clarissa had opted for a three-quarter-length, pleated skirt which matched the colour of her beret.

From her footwear — simple lace-up shoes — it was evident that wherever they were going it would not require them to tackle any strenuous terrain.

Not that there was anything quite like that round here.

Michael had no idea how Clarissa always managed to look so brilliantly individual in this drab and austere post-war Britain, but it made him feel proud and privileged to be walking alongside this unique, beautiful young lady.

'What's on your mind?' he asked after they'd been walking in silence for some considerable way.

Clarissa stopped and turned to face Michael, looking at him as if she had been unaware of his presence until that moment.

'I'm sorry?'

'You seem a little distracted. I thought something must have happened at your house that had upset you.'

'I'm sorry,' Clarissa repeated, but this time it sounded like a genuine apology. 'I'm afraid things had become a bit, well, tense back at my house.

'I just felt the need to go for a walk. A walk,' she added a little too hastily, 'in some congenial company.'

Michael didn't know what to make of all this. If all she'd wanted was a pace-setter or a pet dog, she should have said when she telephoned!

On the other hand, he held the hope that, despite her insularity, he might be able to offer some sort of comfort, if only by being a good listener.

The thought of being nothing more than a substitute for a female friend made him start to feel depressed and he stopped.

Clarissa continued for a few more yards before realising Michael wasn't 'at heel'. She turned back to look at the now stationary figure.

'What's up? Am I going too fast?'

Michael shook his head as he slowly approached Clarissa. Then he contradicted himself.

'Well, yes, in a way you are.' He stopped and faced her. 'I can tell something's wrong, but how am I supposed to know what it is without you telling me?'

Clarissa sighed and looked down.

'It's complicated,' was all she could say.

Now it was Michael's turn to sigh, more from exasperation than anything else.

'Surely it would be less complicated if you were to share it with me.'

They had reached the end of Tennyson Avenue and were facing the busier London-to-Windsor road which separated and divided suburbia from the more open heathland that awaited them on the other side.

It was just a question of getting across. There never seemed to be a big enough gap for them to make the crossing. One side would clear, only for the other carriageway to become busy.

Apart from trades vehicles there were quite a number of motorbikes, many with sidecars, going to and fro.

Suddenly, there was a brief lull. Without thinking, Michael took Clarissa's hand as they dashed across the road to the sanctuary of the open heath with its gorse bushes — always in flower — and the heather still showing a slight haze of its purple colour.

Once over the road Michael tried, reluctantly, to let go of Clarissa's hand. But she held on to his firmly, unwilling to let go, it seemed.

They walked on like this in silence until they reached a place where a stunted pine tree stood.

'Let's sit here,' Clarissa suggested, finally letting go of Michael's hand. 'There's some shade here and we get the view.'

The view was, indeed, worth sitting down for. The heath stretched on for miles, only coming to an end as the

Chepswell hills acted as a green wall to finally enclose it.

Within that boundary, some way off, a line of horseriders were trotting along, off on a hack on this glorious day.

Their steady progress alarmed a lark into voice which continued even after the riders had long since passed.

Michael saw her face relax, as though the sight was having a soothing effect on her troubled mind. If only life could be as simple and peaceful as this scene before them.

'I should have brought a flask,' Michael said, breaking into Clarissa's daydream.

She smiled at him.

'Not to worry, I think we'll survive.'

He knew she was teasing but was glad she felt up to joking.

They sat, still and quiet, for a while longer; long enough for Michael to wonder whether Clarissa had changed her mind about confiding in him.

He wasn't sure how that made him feel. Like Clarissa, he was enjoying the moment, the peace and that sensation of holding Clarissa's hand, even if it was fleeting.

She leaned back against the tree, her head turned skywards and her eyes closed.

'I wish life was always like this,' she said almost to herself.

'It is rather nice,' Michael agreed.

'Nice. Yes.'

Since her mother died and Clarissa had had to leave school and take on all the responsibilities and duties of which Mrs Symons had been in control, it had made her feel older than her years.

Her own life and ambitions had been pushed aside in favour of domesticity.

She was still aware of what she wanted to do in her life but those aspirations were getting further and further away, to the point where, one day, they would have disappeared altogether and she would not even be able to remember what they were.

'You're very quiet,' Michael said.

'I was thinking.'

'What about?'

'This and that; nothing, really.'

'What is it that's troubling you so much — that you were going to tell me?'

Clarissa sighed and opened her eyes. Michael had broken the spell.

'I don't think I should burden you with my problems.'

She grimaced ruefully.

'*My* problems? I wonder why I call them my problems.'

Michael wasn't to be fobbed off again.

'Try telling me about them, Clarissa. It might help.'

A Problem Shared

When Clarissa took Michael's hand it gave him a warm feeling and a sensation of inner strength. Whatever it was that was troubling her, he felt he was equal to sharing the burden and solving it.

Clarissa looked like she was struggling to know where to begin, or how even to explain what was going on.

'I know it's a cliché,' Michael suggested, smiling, 'but it's my understanding that the beginning is usually a good starting point.'

Clarissa tried to smile but it was clear that matters were far too serious.

'I hope we'll still be friends once I've told you.'

Michael didn't know how to take this.

He had been hoping that, at some point in the future — later this afternoon, even — he and Clarissa might become more than friends. His own feelings were already beyond the point of platonic friendship.

This was not a good start.

'Of course we will,' he said, trying to be lighthearted.

'Well,' she finally began, 'it's about my brother and Lorraine, my friend. They've been seeing each other for some time now.

'Then, the other week, Lorraine came round very upset and told me she was pregnant!'

Michael took a deep intake of breath. This was not what he had been expecting to hear.

He had imagined that whatever problem Clarissa was harbouring was hers and hers alone. That, by some means or other, he would be able to help her solve it.

But this? This was beyond his capabilities. He had never known anyone close to him being in this situation before, so he could offer no advice.

'The worst of it is,' Clarissa continued, her voice shaking, 'that Terry's engaged! To Eleanor, Eleanor Tompkins.

'I don't know what to do. Everyone

seems to think that I'll able to sort it out, but how can I?'

She turned to face Michael, a look of appeal in her tear-stained eyes.

Michael let go of her hand and put his arm around her. Clarissa leaned into him, her head resting on his chest.

He found this closeness very distracting: the warmth of her; the nearness; a sensual scent coming from her.

He felt the desire to do more than hold her in his arms.

He wanted to protect her — yes, he wanted to put an end to her concerns.

But most of all he wanted to kiss her, to feel his lips on hers and to feel her giving back to him as much as he was to her.

Meanwhile, he searched for words.

'So obviously no-one else knows yet. Your father, I mean, or Eleanor?'

She shook her head.

'Sometimes, when I can't sleep for thinking about it all, I consider telling them both and then letting them sort it out between them.'

'Why don't you?'

Clarissa sat up but continued to lean against Michael's shoulder.

'I suppose because I think it would be a mean thing to do.'

'But they are going to find out anyway.'

Clarissa nodded and stared into space, silent, imagining the moment where both her father and Eleanor learned of the situation.

'I know, but if I did that I can see everyone turning on me, as though I were somehow to blame!'

'How soon is the baby due?' Michael asked for the sake of breaking the silence.

He knew he wasn't being much use. It was hardly surprising; his mind was still more focused on his desire to kiss Clarissa, as if that would make everything better.

'She's about three months, apparently. But, because Lorrie has always been a bit on the plump side anyway, it's not really showing. Not that it probably would yet.'

'Shouldn't this be Terry's problem?

He is, after all, the father.'

'Yes, he is, and yes, you're right.'

'So?'

'Terry's so immature! So is Lorrie. They're both acting like children and looking to me as the sensible grown up. But I'm not!

'I don't want to have to deal with it. I actually don't know how.

'Also, of course, Terry is away a lot of the time, whereas Lorrie is my constant companion.'

This final remark, concerning her friend, came out sounding sarcastic.

'Well, in my opinion it's too much for you. You shouldn't have to be dealing with this on your own.'

'What do you suggest?' Clarissa asked.

She was looking interested, as if Michael might have an idea worth listening to.

He didn't. But at the same time he wanted to help; he felt the need for Clarissa to be able to rely on him.

All right, if all she needed was a friend right now, then a friend he would be.

'I think,' he began, 'that you must pass the responsibility to where it belongs — to your brother.

'After all, he's the cause of this mess and he has an obligation to his fiancée as much as Lorraine.'

'But he's hardly ever home, and when he is he always finds an excuse to be somewhere else.'

'When is he next on leave?'

'He's got a weekend pass the week after next.'

'Then that's when you must tell him.'

Clarissa looked at her watch. She looked as if she wasn't totally convinced by what Michael had suggested.

He didn't really care. It had still been nice to be in her company; to hold her snuggled up against him and feel the rapid beating of her heart.

'I must go.' She stood up. 'I've got dinner to get ready for when Father comes home.'

Michael stood up, too.

Although his thoughts didn't show in his face, he was feeling annoyed at the apparent hold these other people had over Clarissa.

How unfair it was, he thought. But he said nothing of this as they made their way back.

This time, however, they did not hold hands as they crossed the busy main road.

Nor was there much in the way of conversation as they walked the long, straight length of Tennyson Avenue.

Schoolchildren were starting to appear making their way home; some in groups, some on their own.

It reminded him, and no doubt her, of his own school days.

He had been a bit of a loner, with few friends, though he had not been unpopular. It was just how he was.

Michael remembered Terry, although they had not been in the same year when at school.

Terry had been one of those people who made their presence known. He was popular, an all-rounder at sport and with a personality which even his teachers found endearing.

His sister, on the other hand, as far as he could recall, had been much more single-minded. Not as studious as his own sister, but with an air of determination which showed even back then.

She knew what she was going to do in life; she knew where she was going.

How cruel life can be, Michael decided, that what she had hoped for had been stolen from her through no fault of her own.

'Thanks for coming out with me — and for listening,' Clarissa said as they reached the front gate of her house.

Michael sensed that listening hadn't really been what she had hoped for from him. What Clarissa wanted — needed — were answers.

'I'm afraid I haven't been much use. But at least I feel I am sharing this problem with you.'

He turned to leave, then turned back again.

'I know it may not seem like the right time to say this but I would like to meet up again. For a date.'

That last bit took some courage to say and he wasn't expecting her to agree.

'I'd like that.' She smiled. 'Very much.'

She leaned forward and gave him a light kiss on the cheek.

It didn't signal anything but it gave Michael hope, however misguided it might be.

Grow Up!

Terry duly arrived for his weekend leave, unaware of Clarissa's determination to put the responsibility of his actions firmly in his own hands.

He had looked pleased to be home but also a little concerned to see that Lorraine was at the house again. No doubt it reminded him of things he'd rather not have to be faced with.

Clarissa had arranged for this to happen, without either party knowing that the other one would be here, otherwise neither might have shown up.

On this Saturday afternoon shortly after lunch, with Mr Symons off to play a round of golf at his club, Clarissa invited both Lorraine and Terry into the sitting-room.

'What's up, sis?' Terry wanted to know.

By chance, both he and Lorraine had chosen places together on the sofa whilst Clarissa sat opposite them in one of the armchairs.

'Terry, you know very well what's up. And I want to know exactly what you're going to do about it.

'Have you even discussed matters with Lorraine?'

She watched them both look away from each other and Clarissa, like naughty schoolchildren.

'No, I didn't think so. Well, I'm not carrying your secret any longer!

'Terry, you need to decide what you should do that's right for Lorraine. And Lorraine, you'll have to tell your parents.'

'I can't do that!' Lorraine said, alarmed. 'They'll kill me!'

'Don't be ridiculous. Nobody's going to kill anyone.'

'You don't know my parents.'

Clarissa ignored this remark, turning instead to her brother who, as usual, seemed to have nothing to offer on the subject.

'Terry, I'd be interested to hear what you've got to say.'

'About what?'

Clarissa was flabbergasted.

'About what? About Lorraine being pregnant; about you being engaged! Surely you must have given it some thought.'

'To be honest, I haven't.'

He reached across and took Lorraine's hand.

'No disrespect, Lorrie, but when I'm off doing my National Service I tend to somehow forget everything else.

'I know there's a problem here and it needs to be sorted, but I just don't know how.'

He gave Lorraine's hand a final squeeze, then let it go. It was as if there was nothing else to say — or do.

Again, Clarissa felt the parcel had been passed back to her. But what could she do?

How could she make them both realise the seriousness of their situation and the possibly dreadful consequences?

'I think you both need to grow up and accept responsibility for your actions.'

She turned to Lorraine.

'Soon you won't be able to hide what's

happened. There's a baby on its way and you can't keep it a secret for much longer.'

She turned to her brother.

'You're engaged to be married. How are you going to sort that out?'

Terry shrugged and stood up.

'It'll be all right, you'll see.'

He started to leave the room.

'Where are you going?' Clarissa demanded.

'I'm meeting up with some mates. You can't begrudge me that, surely?'

Before either Clarissa or Lorraine could say anything they heard the front door close behind him.

An Invitation

The post on that Saturday brought an invitation from Eleanor's parents to attend a garden buffet at their home in the village of Moatdene the following day.

Actually, it was more of a reminder to attend, as the official invitation had come two weeks previously.

I do hope you will all come. Eleanor, in particular, is so looking forward to seeing her fiancé again.

'You'll have to go — we all will,' Clarissa told Terry. She could see he was searching for an excuse to avoid going. 'It's not fair on Eleanor!'

'What's not fair on Eleanor?' Mr Symons, who unexpectedly had entered the sitting-room, demanded.

He looked severely at Clarissa despite the fact that the situation was of Terry's making.

'I was just saying to Terry, Father, that it would be such a shame if we all didn't go to the garden party tomorrow.'

'Why on earth wouldn't we go?' Mr Symons responded gruffly.

He turned to his son with a harsher expression on his face.

'It's about time you began behaving responsibly towards that young girl.'

'All right, all right, I'll be going,' Terry insisted defensively. 'You'll be taking us, won't you?'

Mr Symons looked rather taken aback by this. Clearly he felt free to hand out advice without realising that he, too, would be expected to attend.

His hesitation caused Clarissa, unwisely, to speak up.

'You will be expected, too, Father.'

'I know well enough what's expected of me, thank you very much,' he snapped.

He turned and strode out of the room.

'That's settled, then,' Clarissa said drily.

She looked at her brother who, in some world of his own, was gazing blankly out of the window.

She noticed that, despite the extremely

warm weather, ever since his arrival home he had been wearing a jumper over his shirt.

'Have you decided what to wear for tomorrow?' Clarissa asked, wondering how he could bear to be in such unseasonal attire.

Terry looked at her and then down at himself, as if he was only just noticing what he wore.

'What's wrong with this?' he demanded.

'You must be joking! Apart from the fact that today is forecast to be another scorcher, you'll surely need something a bit more suited to summer than winter tomorrow.

'What's more, it doesn't show much consideration for either Mrs Tompkins or Eleanor.'

As she spoke, Clarissa was looking on at herself in an objective way.

A few months ago she could not have imagined herself speaking in this way to her brother!

She seemed to have aged years and

was beginning to act more like a mother — her mother — than she could ever have imagined possible.

It felt as though she'd leapfrogged over youth and headed towards middle age. She didn't care for it.

'I don't have much else, sis. All the fitness training we have to do has added weight and muscles to my body.'

'Well you've still got time to go into town and buy something more appropriate.

'I'll come with you if you'd like,' she added in the hope of encouraging him.

She would enjoy a break herself, even if just to see something other than these four walls.

Terry shook his head.

'No, thanks. The shop will be busy and I'll get fed up with the whole thing.

'Besides, this visit is supposed to be a break for me, Clarissa. The last thing I need is you marching me in and around the shops!'

He started to leave the room.

'Where are you going?' she wanted to know.

'I'm getting a deckchair out. Seems a shame to miss out on this sunshine.'

'You're not going to sunbathe in that jumper?'

Terry didn't reply and left the room.

Clarissa sighed.

There was something going on here that her brother obviously didn't want to discuss.

Wearing that jumper all the time seemed to suggest he was hiding something. But what?

Breakfast Reverie

Sunday dawned with, if anything, even more heat than the previous day. It could only end in a thunderstorm but, hopefully, that wouldn't happen today.

Clarissa was, as ever, the first one in the household to rise.

She had struggled to get to sleep, partly because of the heat which, despite having her bedroom window open, would not lessen.

There was something else keeping her awake and it had nothing to do with the weather. Although, indirectly, it did.

She was still troubled by her brother's strange reluctance to not remove that revolting jumper, as well as by his apparent indifference to all the urgent issues that were crowding in on him. And, as a result, on her.

Downstairs in the kitchen Clarissa began preparations for breakfast.

The clock showed it was ten past seven and the sun was streaming in through the window.

At least, at this time of year, there was no need of a fire. That allowed Clarissa the indulgence of her own pot of tea before setting out the breakfast things in the dining-room.

The tea, despite the weather, was surprisingly refreshing, and it allowed Clarissa a moment's respite, giving her time to think of herself for a change.

She still intended, one day, to follow her dream of being an artist but the domesticity that was now her life still encroached on that ambition.

What had surprised her, however, was how certain aspects of her new, changed life had brought out another side to her creative talents.

There was the garden and also cookery. She had surprised herself by how much pleasure she had derived from both these occupations.

From growing the ingredients for her meals to cooking the meals themselves, Clarissa had discovered that not all creativity began and ended with a paintbrush.

Joy of joys, even her father had had, uncharacteristically, occasion to comment favourably on some of her more adventurous recipes.

Then there was Michael. His intrusion into her thoughts was both welcome and disturbing.

She had agreed to go out — officially — with him on a date. He had suggested the cinema where a film called 'The Young Lovers' had recently been released.

Clarissa couldn't recall the last time she'd watched a film. It would be extremely pleasant to be able to watch how other people dealt with their problems, rather than her own.

In addition, the thought of sitting next to Michael in a cosy, dimly lit atmosphere gave her goosebumps in spite of the heat, which was already building up.

This realisation took her thoughts away from that warm, enveloping feeling to considerations of what on earth it was that was going on with her brother.

More specifically, what was he going

to wear today for their visit to the Tompkinses?

He could hardly turn up looking like a tramp. Mr and Mrs Tompkins had, if anything, even higher standards than Clarissa's own mother.

She was aware that Terry's affections had now, to some extent, transferred themselves to Lorraine.

That made it even more important that he should face up to his responsibilities and make a decision to do whatever was best in these confusing circumstances.

'Hi, sis, any tea in that pot?'

Clarissa turned, to see her brother standing in the doorway, his dressing-gown tied loosely over his pyjamas.

'Talk of the devil,' she said. 'I was just thinking about you.'

'All good, I hope.' He grinned in that appealing way that made even Clarissa's heart melt in affection for her brother.

'It's going to be another scorcher,' she said, standing up to get him a cup and saucer from the dresser.

'Should suit me, then.'

He continued to smile as he sat down at the large, scrubbed kitchen table, awaiting his tea which Clarissa now poured.

She was aware, as she passed the full cup to him, how difficult it was for a girl to be seen in any way other than someone whose main purpose in life was to serve men.

This awareness was highlighted by her own brother's apparent willingness to perpetuate the custom.

If someone of her own generation saw her in this subservient light, what hope had she of competing in the male-dominated world of work?

'Penny for them,' Terry said.

Clarissa sat down but kept a close watch on the time. Father would be up soon.

He'd wash and shave first, then get dressed before coming down to his breakfast of two soft-boiled eggs and toast.

'I was thinking I must get on. Father will be wanting his breakfast.'

Terry shrugged.

'Let him wait. Give yourself a break. You're always on the go.'

'OK,' she countered, 'you get his breakfast, then! Don't forget he likes his eggs boiled for exactly three and a half minutes.'

She made to stand up, suggesting she was about to leave the room.

Alarmed, Terry leaped from his chair, causing it to fall to the floor behind him.

'Where are you going?' His voice held panic.

Clarissa stopped.

'Sorry? I thought you wanted to help. Am I mistaken?'

Terry picked up the chair.

'Very funny. I'll let you get on. I'm off to get ready.'

That should be interesting, Clarissa thought.

She had half a mind to go and grab that old jumper of his and put it in with the rest of tomorrow's wash.

But the moment passed — there was the small matter of a couple of eggs to be boiled.

The Garden Party

Mr Symons drove his Standard 8 along the byways which would eventually lead them to the rather grand drive of Hathaway House, home of the Tompkins family.

In this area the dwellings did not have numbers, only names, which supposedly gave them a higher status.

The two gryphons mounted on either side of the walled entrance (purchased from a salvage reclamation yard though originally from a former stately home) gave the mock-Tudor house a certain gravitas as far as Mrs Tompkins was concerned.

There were already quite a number of cars parked, which didn't pass unnoticed by Terry, seated beside his father.

'Who are all these people?'

Clarissa leaned forward to see.

'Gosh, don't they look smart!' she said, aware more of the outfits than the numbers.

She glanced across to what her brother was wearing. He'd compromised a little — the jumper was gone and had been replaced with a smarter, tailored cream shirt and newly pressed cavalry twill trousers.

It was a definite improvement but she couldn't help but notice how he kept tugging at the shirt cuffs.

Mr Symons parked his car a little way off from the others, perhaps feeling it inappropriate for his small saloon to stand alongside the Armstrong Siddeleys and Vauxhall Wyverns which dominated here.

At the door, both Mr and Mrs Tompkins were waiting to greet the arriving guests.

'How lovely to see you!' Mrs Tompkins gushed. 'All of you,' she emphasised, giving her future son-in-law an old-fashioned look.

'Where is Eleanor?' Clarissa asked, feeling that someone — if not Terry — should make reference to her brother's fiancée.

'She'll be in the garden, organising the caterers. I felt I needed to give her something to occupy herself with...'

Her voice trailed off as her eyes moved from Clarissa to Terry once more.

'Go on through.' She beckoned with a gesture that seemed more dismissive than welcoming.

They made their way through the wide hallway, where great sprays of flowers stood on plinths, and out through the back sitting-room. Its French windows opened on to the terrace which stood a few steps above the large manicured garden.

The Symons family group was offered drinks by a smartly dressed waiter at the top of the steps. Each took one as they made their way down to the lawn, where other tables were set out with plates and canapés.

There was a small marquee erected in case the weather suddenly broke. At the moment there was no sign of that happening; the sun enjoyed total dominance in a clear blue sky.

Some people — mainly those who were hatless — were taking shelter in the marquee or standing under the larger specimen trees which offered welcome shade.

Clarissa looked all around her as she sipped her wine. She was on the look-out for Eleanor and was curious to see what her brother's reaction and response would be when she appeared.

As it was, it took them both by surprise. Two youthful, manicured hands were placed over Terry's eyes from behind.

One of them displayed, on the appropriate finger, a diamond engagement ring.

'Guess who!' the voice said.

Terry gently removed Eleanor's hands as he turned to face her.

'Hi,' he said with a weak smile.

Eleanor frowned.

'Hi? Is that all I get after all this time?'

She walked sulkily away. Clarissa nudged her brother, who had remained motionless as Eleanor stormed off.

'For goodness' sake, Terry, go after her!'

Terry glanced at Clarissa, clearly considering for a moment what she had told him to do.

With a sigh he walked slowly off in the direction that Eleanor had gone.

Clarissa had to force herself not to follow. She reminded herself that this was not her problem, although it had seemed to be hers from the moment Lorraine had called round with her devastating news.

She longed to wander around the large garden, to make a closer inspection on the types of flowers and shrubs that the Tompkins family favoured for their beds and borders.

Clarissa realised how resigned she was to her situation by the fact that she was already planning what to sow and grow next year.

Her father looked all at sea in this social gathering. Since the death of his wife he'd avoided any sort of company other than that which was necessary.

He'd resigned his post at the local freemasons' lodge, which was a disappointment to Clarissa as it gave her even less privacy or opportunity to let her hair down.

She longed to play some of her records on the family radiogram but there was never a chance to do so.

'Shall I get you another drink, Father?' she asked, feeling guilty even though her father would have no idea of what had been going on in her mind.

Mr Symons ignored the offer. He was too busy looking all around him as if searching for someone.

'Where's he gone to now?' he eventually asked.

'Who? Do you mean Terry?'

Again there came that irritation at whatever Clarissa had to say.

'Of course I mean Terry! Who else would I mean?'

Clarissa chose once again to ignore her parent's ill temper.

'I think he went off with Eleanor somewhere.'

A silence fell between them; it seemed there was nothing more to say.

Too Hot for Comfort

It was with some reluctance that Terry followed Eleanor as she made her way back towards the house. The closer he got to her, he realised, the closer his problems were getting.

Never one to face up to his responsibilities, he was realising this was a situation which nobody else could fix.

In fact, it was one which couldn't be put right without a lot of unpleasantness.

Eleanor had reached the terrace and was sitting on one of the patio chairs. Despite the steely expression on her face there were traces of tears, which only added to Terry's discomfort.

'Eleanor,' he began as he reached her. 'What did you run off for?'

He put out his hand in an attempt to take hers but Eleanor was having none of it, folding her arms tightly.

The gesture having failed, and getting no response to his question, Terry went and lifted one of the other chairs on the patio, parking it next to her before, gingerly, sitting down himself.

'I'm sorry if I've upset you, Eleanor,' he began.

'What do you mean, *if* you've upset me?' she countered. 'And what's with all this Eleanor stuff? Have I become such a stranger to you?'

Terry realised belatedly that he had not used the more personal and endearing term of Ellipops. But it would not sit well on his tongue any more.

'I'm sorry,' was all he could say.

She looked at his clothes.

'Why would you come here looking like this, anyway?' she demanded. 'It's the hottest day of the year, yet you're done up as if it's chilly.

'You can at least roll your sleeves up so you don't draw attention to yourself.'

She moved nearer to him. There was a softer expression on her face as if she wanted to make up.

Terry was having none of it. He tried to stand up but Eleanor was too quick for him. He was frozen in place, unable to prevent Eleanor from rolling up his sleeves playfully.

The impish grin on her face changed firstly to bewilderment and then to fury. 'What on earth is this?'

Terry's Secret

The journey home was as atmospheric as the storm that was about to break above the family.

As usual, Mr Symons said nothing. It was possible he may have been relieved at their sudden departure from the Tompkins's garden party.

He certainly didn't wait for explanations, just got in the car and, with his children on board, drove off.

Although Clarissa was only able to look at the back of her brother's head, she could not glean anything from it. She was as stunned as anyone.

'We need to go,' Terry had told her, running up and looking around like a hunted animal. 'Get Father. We need to go. Now!'

Clarissa had discovered Mr Symons dozing off in a chair by a rose bed.

'Father!' she had all but whispered. She had touched his arm gently. 'Terry says we need to go.'

She looked up at the sky.

'I think there's a storm coming; you won't want to be driving in the pouring rain.'

Mr Symons had stirred slowly from his snooze, the passive expression on his face altering to the familiar frown which he seemed to reserve for his daughter.

'What are you saying? Speak up, girl.'

'Terry thinks we ought to go, Father. It could rain any minute, and you know you don't like driving in the rain.'

She'd held out her hand to offer assistance, but he'd ignored the gesture, slowly lifting himself out of the chair.

'I suppose we should thank our hosts,' he'd told her without conviction.

'That won't be necessary, Father. Terry's already done that.'

A lie. Something which Clarissa was not used to doing. But it was probably going to be just the first of many from now on.

A look of immense relief had registered on Mr Symons's face.

'Right, let's be off, then.'

And now they were heading home.

Terry, no doubt aware of his sister's scrutiny, turned to look at Clarissa, a hint of a smile on his lips.

Clarissa instinctively returned the smile, even though her heart felt heavy with what must have taken place and all that she didn't, as yet, know about.

What exactly had happened to cause their sudden departure? Why had Eleanor run off, sobbing uncontrollably?

Why had Mrs Tompkins called Terry an absolute swine, and why hadn't Terry defended himself?

These were all questions that needed answering although, at the same time, Clarissa dreaded discovering the truth.

They arrived back home shortly before three.

It was at moments like these that Clarissa wished she had a dog. Any sort of breed, even a mongrel.

Anything to give her a justifiable excuse to get out of the house, to go off somewhere where her only consideration would be for the welfare of a pet dog.

She had broached the subject just once to her father, but he wouldn't hear of it.

Terry headed for the garage where his motorbike was stored.

'Where are you going?' Clarissa wanted to know.

Terry stopped and turned to face her. 'I need to clear my head. Come with me,' he beckoned.

Because she was feeling so much in need of some sort of escape, she agreed, even though the source of the problem would be going with her.

The storm which had been threatening for a good part of the afternoon didn't materialise, at least in Chepswell, so as the motorbike raced it was good to feel the breeze streaming through Clarissa's hair and caressing her face.

She felt a thrill of excitement as they sped along empty lanes and had every confidence in Terry's ability to keep them both safe.

She didn't even care where they were going; at this moment she could have stayed riding indefinitely to keep getting further away from all her problems.

Eventually Terry pulled into a lay-by. Once the engine was switched off Clarissa was almost overwhelmed by the sudden silence.

There was not a bird singing; not another car or motorbike to be heard. It seemed strange and, for no reason which she could explain, unwelcome.

Terry sat on the grass and took a packet of cigarettes from his trouser pocket.

'I didn't know you smoked!' Clarissa said, surprised.

Terry smiled, blowing smoke out as he did.

'Well, sis, just goes to show you don't know everything about me.'

'I never said I did.' She joined him on the grass.

Terry offered her a puff on his cigarette but she shook her head.

'Something else I don't know,' she countered, pulling at tufts of grass, 'is what happened between you and Eleanor that had us going home all of a sudden.'

By way of answer Terry rolled up his sleeve on his right arm.

Clarissa cried out in shock.

'You showed that to Eleanor?' was all she could find to say. What Terry had just revealed was astonishing.

'I didn't deliberately show it to her; she found it all by herself, pulling my shirtsleeves up.'

Although there was still a little scabbing left on the tattoo you could, nevertheless, clearly make out a heart with a scroll going round it, and the name Lorraine set into it.

Clarissa shook her head.

'I can't believe it. What were you thinking of?'

Terry shrugged.

'We were out for the evening, me and a few of the lads. To cut a long story short, I had a bit too much to drink and decided — as you do — to have a tattoo done.'

'Just like that?'

Clarissa was still not able to believe what she was hearing and seeing.

'And it had to be Lorraine, not your fiancée, Eleanor?'

Terry sighed, stubbing his cigarette out on the grass.

'I suppose the alcohol had brought out my true feelings.'

'Feelings?'

'Yes. That I no longer felt I could marry Eleanor.'

'But you didn't think to tell her this? You had to let her find out in the cruellest and most tasteless way!'

Clarissa felt so angry with her brother, at his total lack of feeling for how devastated Eleanor must be at this moment.

It was humiliating as well as shocking.

She also realised that, in her brother's explanation, he had failed to say that he loved Lorraine.

'You know your problem, Terry? You only care about yourself. As long as you don't get hurt by your actions, then that's all right. Only this time it isn't!'

★ ★ ★

Terry wouldn't meet his sister's eyes; he could not honestly admit that she was wrong in her accusations.

He did love Lorraine; the trouble was that he was also, for the first time in a very long time, loving life.

Doing his National Service had given him something real to aspire to that would be of his own making.

He enjoyed the camaraderie which he'd discovered; he also enjoyed the unquestioning friendliness that others in his platoon offered. It was the closest he'd come to really experiencing what he would consider family life.

Apart from all that, being in the Army had opened up for Terry a whole new world of travel and adventure, a world he'd only heard of before and which he desired, very much, to further explore.

It was the Army that was giving him this opportunity.

Yes, of course there were risks — what was life without risks? A lot duller, Terry knew, reflecting on his previous existence on Civvy Street.

* * *

'You're not saying anything again, I notice.'

Clarissa needed some sort of response from her brother, if only to lift the unasked-for weight of responsibility from her own young shoulders.

'I don't know what to say, sis. I know I've made a mistake and I want to sort it out, but I can't see my way through.'

Clarissa was not intending to offer her brother sympathy; she had run out of any reserves for that.

She did feel, however, that she needed him to make a decision regarding the mess he'd got everyone into, and to make it soon.

Time was not on anyone's side.

'When do you go back to barracks?' she asked instead as a thought hit her.

Terry frowned.

'I have to be back by nine a.m. Tomorrow, that is. Why do you ask?'

Clarissa stood up, brushing any loose grass off her clothes.

'Right, then, that means you've got from now till early tomorrow morning to sort this out once and for all.

'Come on.'

She started to walk towards Terry's motorbike.

'Where are we going?'

'To Lorraine's,' she told him without looking back.

Breaking the News

There were so many things to arrange. The easiest of these was breaking off the engagement between Terry and Eleanor.

Actually, it was Eleanor who did the breaking, by letter with the engagement ring enclosed.

The last thing she wanted, clearly, was her name and her family's name dragged through the courts with a case for breach of promise. That was something the local paper would have relished.

Not so straightforward was explaining to Lorraine's parents about their daughter's 'condition' and then explaining it for a second time to Terry's father.

There were some unholy scenes, as the late Mrs Symons might have described it.

Lorraine's parents obviously blamed Terry, but their own daughter did not escape their fury and disappointment.

In the end, of course, they recognised that the only way of avoiding a scandal was to give their permission for Lorraine to marry Terry.

He himself had tried to introduce certain provisos into the forthcoming union. One of them was that he intended to remain in the Army. He would be posted to a base in Germany.

No-one, least of all Lorraine, was happy about this.

'It's probably for the best to start with,' Clarissa told her friend encouragingly when Lorraine called round to her friend's house for the umpteenth time, handkerchief in hand.

'But I don't want to have a baby in Germany! It's not right.'

'You'll be on a British Army base; it will be just the same as being at home.'

Clarissa had no idea where she got these reassuring remarks from. She had no more idea of what it would be like for a young girl in a foreign country than Lorraine did herself.

But she felt she must try and paint a positive picture for her.

'I shall miss you so much, Clarry!' was

all Lorraine had to say as the tears began to pour again.

Wedding Plans

Michael Parkes was feeling left out in the cold. The pre-arranged visit to the cinema, to see 'The Young Lovers' with Clarissa, had been put off.

On the postcard sent to him last Monday had been a brief apology but no explanation as to why.

What he suspected, but hoped was not true, was that she had changed her mind about him as a possible boyfriend.

That she was not attracted to him, and, furthermore, she now regretted confiding in him some of her troubles when they'd been together on that walk.

Michael had no excuse, either, to make contact with her. He could hardly hang around the churchyard on the off chance of 'bumping' into her as she attended her mother's grave.

And time was running out. He had received notice of his posting, up in the highlands of Scotland. Could it have been further away?

He fully accepted the need for him to go and serve his country, as his father had gladly done. He also hoped that his learned skills as a chef might offer some useful and fulfilling service both to the RAF and himself.

He just wished there was more time, and that he could think of an excuse for seeing Clarissa once more before leaving.

But perhaps it was better to accept that Clarissa was never going to be any more than a friend, and to move to Scotland.

* * *

Clarissa, meanwhile, was wondering if she'd been too hasty in cancelling her outing to the cinema with Michael.

At the time of writing the postcard there seemed to be so much pressing on her mind and so many things to do.

But her own organisational skills had turned a potential catastrophe almost into a triumph. Lorraine's parents were gradually coming to terms with the situation, accepting that even a registry-office wedding was better than no wedding at all.

'We must keep the Press out of it,' Maud Cutler had told her daughter. As if her daughter's situation was the sort of thing that might end up in the 'News Of The World'.

Lorraine pointed out that it could only get as far as the local paper if you actually requested one of the 'Gazette's' photographers to come and take your wedding photo for their *Marriage Lines* page.

It had been straightforward getting the registry office booked, but not quite as easy for Terry to get leave in order to get married.

'It's the Army that you're married to, Symons,' his commanding officer reminded him.

It was fortunate that Mrs Symons was no longer alive to hear the pronunciation of her son's surname as used by the military.

Terry hadn't dared to correct his superior officers when they chose to call him 'Sighmons'. In some ways he preferred it — it gave him, obscurely, a sort of individual personality that he hadn't really had before.

In the end, the Army gave him a 72-hour pass for the weekend of November 20, coincidentally the same date as Queen Elizabeth's wedding anniversary.

This last fact went some way in placating Lorraine's mother.

Geoffrey Symons was less easily impressed, but didn't care much, either. The less disruption to his life the better.

Better still was that his daughter, it seemed, was taking care of most of it.

The one thing he had conceded to, grudgingly, was allowing a sort of reception to take place at his home.

Again, Lorraine's mother felt a need to make the whole wedding some sort of covert operation. The further away from her own home it took place, the better.

'What about a cake?' Clarissa asked

her friend when Lorraine called round to see her.

'That would be nice, thank you,' Lorraine replied, completely misunderstanding the question.

Clarissa hadn't been offering to make one. She didn't really know how, plus there were still shortages for everyday food items, let alone for something as elaborate as a wedding cake.

But it seemed there was no way out of it. Lorraine's expression had changed to such a joyful one that Clarissa felt it would be cruel to dash her hopes.

'I'll see what I can do.'

'It doesn't have to be too fancy,' Lorraine said.

Trust me, it won't be, Clarissa thought.

This business of a wedding cake brought Michael to her mind. He was now a fully trained chef, she knew, and probably had a much better idea than she of how to make a cake using limited ingredients.

But, of course, she'd spoiled things by

sending him that terse postcard.

Surely, she tried to reason with herself, in a situation like this he would be only too pleased — maybe even flattered — to help.

It was worth a try.

* * *

'Oh, dear,' Clarissa said, ineffectually as she spoke to Michael's mother on the telephone.

'Yes, it was all a bit sudden. Michael seemed pleased to be going, though,' she added, as if that might make it easier to accept.

'Well, yes.' Clarissa did not know what else to say.

'Was there any particular reason you were calling, er . . . ?'

'Clarissa. No, no. Just to wish him well.'

'Well, I'll certainly pass on your good wishes, although it will be some time before we'll even be hearing from him, let alone seeing him.'

The call ended. Clarissa very slowly and gently lowered the handset back on to its cradle. She was more shocked and upset than she could have imagined on hearing that Michael was gone.

She was starting to understand what Michael had come to mean to her. And it had nothing to do with baking.

Wedding Day

The weeks that led up to the wedding proved to be busy ones both for Clarissa and Lorraine.

Despite not having a traditional church wedding, Lorraine still wanted to look like a bride. This demanded some creativity from both her and Clarissa.

Each searched out remnants from their own homes and, with the help of Mrs Symons's redundant sewing-machine, they managed to produce a reasonable and stylish, two-piece outfit in a greyish lime-coloured material.

A hat was more of a problem. In the end they had to go to Aldenhams, the large department store in Chepswell, to purchase one that best matched Lorraine's costume.

'What about you, Clarry? Won't you need one?'

The thought hadn't occurred to Clarissa; she had been so busy organising everyone else that she'd not taken into consideration her own needs.

'Do you think I will? I've only got my beret. I could wear my old school boater, mind,' she added mischievously.

Lorraine grinned. That brought comfort to Clarissa, seeing her friend so buoyed up by the forthcoming event.

Things could have easily gone the other way, causing misery and heartache. This was so much better and Clarissa found herself caught up in Lorraine's enthusiasm.

'Look, while we're here let's have a coffee in the restaurant.'

She saw Lorraine look at her watch.

'It's all right, they'll have finished doing the lunches by now. Come on.'

She took Lorraine's arm and led the way to the rooftop restaurant which offered a panoramic view across the town and beyond to the Chepswell hills.

As they sat down at a table close by to the window, Clarissa looked out across this view. For some inexplicable reason she felt sadness tug at her heart.

'You all right, Clarry?' Lorraine leaned

across and put her hand on her friend's arm.

Clarissa managed to brush away a tear before turning back.

'Just something in my eye,' she said.

★ ★ ★

Geoffrey Symons wasn't going to be rushed by anyone, least of all his daughter. 'I'll be ready when I'm ready,' he told her, still seated at the breakfast table and hiding, as ever, behind his copy of the 'Daily Telegraph'.

'I'm just a bit concerned there may be a lot of traffic, Father, what with it being Saturday.'

Mr Symons didn't respond to his daughter's appeal. In fact, he had hardly responded in any positive way to the wedding about to take place.

As usual, it was Clarissa who was in the firing line for his disapproval. There was no-one else at home.

It was very wearing, as it was, no doubt, intended to be. Her father wanted a compliant, unquestioning daughter, someone without ambition or personality.

If Clarissa had been of a weaker spirit that might have very well been what he'd have got. But it was both hard and unfair to be always in this position.

It was left to Terry to get his father moving.

'Come on, Dad, we don't want to be late. Well, I don't, anyway!'

Clarissa had noticed many differences in her brother since he'd joined the Army, not least of which was his referring to his father as 'Dad'.

Whether Mr Symons had failed to notice the shift from the more formal form of address to this much more familiar term was not evident in his responses.

It was just another sign of things changing — of Terry shifting away from his own family background. Yes, Terry was moving on, and gladly, whereas Clarissa was still tied up in harbour, so to speak.

An empty vessel. The expression came

to mind and it didn't please her to think that that was how she was beginning to see herself.

There wasn't even Michael around to encourage her to think more of herself.

But, she told herself, that was of no importance, today of all days. There was a wedding taking place.

All the omens were good. It was unseasonably warm and sunny, making Clarissa think it was in some way due to it also being the Queen's anniversary.

Whatever it was, it certainly made a difference as to how people would look upon the occasion and its participants.

'I wonder how Lorraine's feeling,' Terry said to his sister once Mr Symons had slowly, reluctantly, put down his paper and left the room.

'I expect she's a bit nervous — excited, as well. How are you feeling? You seem quite relaxed about it all.'

Terry grinned.

'Not really. I've got a bagful of butterflies in my stomach. It all seems a little unreal, don't you think?'

'It'll feel real enough when the baby comes along!'

Terry's smile vanished.

'Thanks for reminding me, sis.'

Clarissa, not for the first time, felt concern regarding her brother's feelings towards his bride-to-be. He had never openly expressed his love for Lorraine — not to Clarissa, anyway.

But he must love her. After all, he got a tattoo done of her, even though he'd had a few drinks at the time. And he no longer made any attempt to conceal it.

There had been a few words exchanged between father and son over the matter but, somehow, the way Terry stood up to his parent seemed to make him stronger.

Clarissa wondered what the reaction would be if she got a tattoo done herself. Not that she would seriously consider such a move.

The thought came from the desperate need she had to be noticed, as a person in her own right.

Her vivid imagination briefly pictured the image — a heart, similar to Terry's.

Then, to her shock, she imagined Michael's name in the scroll around it.

'Are you OK, sis? You've gone all silent and dreamy.'

Clarissa smiled.

'I'm fine. Let's get ready or there'll be no wedding to go to.'

Terry went to say something but then seemed to think better of it.

★ ★ ★

The marriage ceremony was a sad affair, really. Clarissa imagined it was probably like many such weddings that took place, hurriedly, during the war.

This idea was given more credence by the fact that Terry was wearing his Army uniform and that Lorraine was pregnant, also by the small number attending.

Outside, she ran ahead to sprinkle the newlyweds with some confetti but it seemed rather futile.

Thank goodness we didn't ask the 'Gazette' to come and photograph this, she thought, looking at the strained expressions on just about everybody's face.

Terry's father took the wedding pair back to his house in his Standard 8 with, for once, Clarissa sitting in front.

The last time a female had been privileged enough to be in this position was when the late Mrs Symons sat here.

Terry and Lorraine sat close together, occasionally smiling at one another and squeezing hands.

Lorraine's purpose in clinging on to Terry was twofold. Apart from the relief of being made 'an honest woman' despite her teenage years, she found her father-in-law's driving a bit nerve-racking.

He seemed to think that the road belonged to him and him alone; other users were in his way and to be swerved past, usually with a resounding blast on his horn.

Clarissa felt equally petrified but found it easier if, for the most part, she closed her eyes and hoped for the best. After all, her father drove to and from work daily and no harm had come to him or others.

Lorraine's parents arrived in their own Hillman a few minutes after the Standard 8 pulled into the drive of The Cedars. Terry offered to carry Lorraine over the threshold but his new wife declined, partly through embarrassment and partly because this was not their home.

Once everyone was assembled in the living-room a few drinks were poured and a toast offered to Terry and Lorraine who stood awkwardly together whilst their health and happiness were being toasted.

'Shall I put a record on?' Clarissa asked, feeling brave in this company.

Before anyone could object, Terry replied.

'Great idea, sis. What have you got?'

There wasn't a great deal to choose from. Quite a few Mantovani and Semprini discs, but also, incongruously, a single record by Frank Sinatra — 'Love And Marriage'.

Clarissa wondered how it had got

here. Not in her mother's time, that was for sure.

Terry wouldn't have bought it, either. That sort of music didn't interest him.

That left Clarissa's father, although the idea of Mr Symons going to a record shop and buying a romantic single was not something that Clarissa could picture.

Still, he had been going out quite a bit just lately in the evenings, never saying to where or with whom. She'd noticed a certain amount of preening at the mirrored hallstand before he stepped out, a definite lightness in both his manner and his gait.

Could he have been seeing someone?

The question remained unanswered as she placed the record on to the turntable and lowered the needle.

'Love and marriage,' she murmured as the music began. 'Do the two always go together?'

An Impending Crisis

Nearly eight months had passed since Terry and Lorraine had got married. Now in married quarters in Germany, with Terry having signed up for five years, they were the proud parents of a baby girl, Helen.

Clarissa had seen photographs but that was all. Her father made no mention of them and Clarissa thought it best not to encourage him.

He seemed to have other things on his mind lately. In contrast to his behaviour the previous year, Mr Symons appeared to have discovered a new lease of life.

His manner towards Clarissa had not fundamentally changed and he was still mostly disapproving of Terry — not so much for marrying Lorraine as for giving up his job at the bank — but there was something going on.

Instead of coming in from work, eating his dinner and then listening to the wireless whilst doing the crossword, as often as not he would smarten himself up before going out for the evening, leaving in his wake a waft of Old Spice.

He never said where he was going, nor did she consider asking. But it puzzled her.

Concerning her more was what was going on thousands of miles away in Egypt. The Suez Crisis, as the newspapers were calling it, was reaching the point where Armed-Forces intervention by the British was becoming ever more likely.

Terry, now a corporal, would be one of those deployed to that trouble spot, as might Michael, currently stationed somewhere in Scotland.

He had written a couple of times but Clarissa had not responded. Not because she didn't want to, but because she was unable to see further than each day and its relevance to her.

She liked Michael a lot. He was kind and considerate, and very good looking, too. But she had seen how love could complicate things and she lacked the courage to risk her own emotions, when there was no guarantee that it would turn out well for her.

She still held the hope that, one day, she would achieve her ambition of being an artist in her own right. The less involved she was in someone else's life and ambitions the easier it would be for her to achieve her own.

But she struggled to convince herself that this was true.

Tea and Halibut

One dull November morning there came a knock at the door of number 48.

Clarissa answered, thinking it might be the postman, but it wasn't. It was Michael, smartly attired in his RAF uniform.

'Good morning, Clarissa,' he said.

'Michael!' Clarissa didn't know which sensation, surprise or pleasure, was the greater. 'How nice. Come in.'

As she stood back to let Michael enter she became painfully aware how inappropriately she was dressed for his visit.

Clothes were still difficult enough to come by. Besides, she'd mostly lost interest in her appearance; the drudgery of domesticity hardly encouraged a preoccupation of fashion in her own life.

Michael's arrival reminded her she ought to make an effort for her own sake.

'Go through to the sitting-room.' She pointed, then headed for the kitchen. 'I'll make tea, or would you prefer coffee?'

'Tea would be fine.'

* * *

Michael walked into the sitting-room, already feeling that things were not going as he'd hoped. By sending him off in here she was treating him as a guest, no more than that.

In his imagination he had pictured a totally different reunion — one where they rushed into each other's arms, kissing long and passionately.

After this they would have both sat close together in the kitchen, having jointly made the drinks, sharing this simple act of domesticity.

He was still standing, with his back to the window, when Clarissa came in. She was carrying a tray on which was a teapot, jug of hot water, milk, sugar and a small plate of assorted biscuits.

This was not what Michael had expected. He could be anyone, it seemed, and the treatment would be the same.

'Here, let me take that for you.'

He came forward to take the tray off Clarissa but she was already at the occasional table.

As they both leaned in towards one another they just managed — awkwardly — to avoid banging heads.

'Sorry,' Michael muttered, stepping back again.

He was already feeling that his visit was a mistake.

It had been unfair of him to turn up unannounced, perhaps, but he'd been desperate to see Clarissa and had had high hopes of this encounter.

* * *

Clarissa was feeling awkward, hot and nervous. She felt ashamed to be seen in these workaday clothes, complete with unflattering housecoat. And her hair was in a turban, as was a common custom with housewives these days.

What must he be thinking of her, she wondered.

'Sit down, Michael.'

She began to pour the tea.

Michael sat opposite, concentrating

on the tea pouring, seeming unwilling to meet Clarissa's eyes.

He, too, looked awkward and hot. Perhaps he was regretting having turned up unannounced like this. No doubt he could tell it was making Clarissa feel uncomfortable.

★ ★ ★

Had she known it, Michael was considering how soon he could possibly take his leave without causing offence.

'How are you finding life in the RAF?' Clarissa asked, sitting back in her armchair, her cup of tea in her hand. 'Do help yourself to a biscuit. I made them myself.'

Michael was surprised.

'Really?'

Clarissa laughed.

'No, not really.'

He realised she was trying to lighten the mood; to make things appear 'normal' between them.

'Well, if that's the case, I will have

one.' Michael grinned. Like Clarissa, he longed to make the visit less formal, less conventional.

Clarissa smiled back. There was warmth in it and it melted Michael's heart to see that preoccupied, anxious look disappear — if briefly — from her beautiful face.

It changed his mind there and then about leaving at the earliest opportunity. He wanted to stay for ever, just to take her in his arms and kiss away all her troubles and tiredness.

'What are you thinking? You look miles away,' she said.

Michael pulled himself together, fearing that Clarissa might have realised what he had been thinking.

'Anyway,' she said, once it became clear that Michael was not going to answer her question. 'Tell me what you can about how and what you're doing.'

'Actually, there's not much to say. There's an awful lot of repetition in what we do, and an awful lot of shouting, too!'

There was that smile again. If she only knew the effect it was having on him.

'What I do like, though, is Scotland. Have you ever been there?'

Clarissa shook her head.

'No, it's mostly been Torquay for us, unfortunately. And Italy once, long ago.'

'Well, Torquay's not so bad. Mind you, I don't imagine it has quite the wildness of Scotland.'

Again Clarissa smiled, although he saw her tuck wayward strands of hair under the turban as though ashamed.

Had she but known it, Michael thought that she looked even more beautiful like this. Her hair being hidden inside the turban showed the clear, classic beauty of the young woman's face.

'I'm sure you would like it in Scotland,' Michael continued. 'The mountains, the wildlife and the weather are all asking to be painted.'

From her lack of response to this observation Michael could see that he had, inadvertently, upset Clarissa.

She looked away from him.

'I've more or less given up on painting,' she told him.

Her eyes fell on a framed photograph on the sideboard. It had been taken on holiday in Torquay by one of those professional photographers who were for ever touting for trade along the promenade.

It depicted Clarissa and her brother standing in front of their parents. Everyone was smiling.

It had been taken in or around 1946 and to all appearances they seemed a happy family.

Clarissa's mother, in particular, wore a relaxed, beaming expression which showed how attractive she had been. Even Mr Symons seemed happy.

But, then, Michael reflected, this was just a snapshot in a lifetime. Photographs rarely showed how things were beneath the surface.

'Was that Torquay?'

Clarissa quickly looked back at him and nodded.

'Do you fancy a walk?' she asked impulsively, standing up as she spoke.

Michael glanced out of the window. It wasn't the most inviting weather for a walk.

Clarissa followed his gaze and immediately sat down again.

'Silly idea,' she muttered, shaking her head.

'No, no. Sorry. I'd love to go for a walk, really I would.'

'It's all right, Michael, you don't have to humour me. I just feel . . . well, I don't know how I feel.'

Then, before he knew it, he found himself saying what, for all this time, his heart had wanted her to hear.

'I know how I feel, Clarissa, and I've wanted to tell you for some time now. I love you.'

He stood up and approached her slowly, as though fearful of frightening her off. As if she were a wild creature, mistrustful of humans.

He kneeled down in front of her, taking both her hands in his.

She smiled nervously but didn't remove her hands.

'You're not going to propose, are you?'

'I would if I thought you'd say yes,' he replied.

Just then the telephone rang.

'I'd better get that,' Clarissa said.

Michael got to his feet awkwardly, Clarissa all but stepping over him to get to the phone.

It was making the moment before a bit of a farce.

Michael stood in the room, listening as Clarissa spoke to the fishmonger.

He was explaining that they didn't have any halibut but perhaps the smoked haddock would do.

If it hadn't been for the fact that the telephone was situated in the hall, Michael might have thought of slipping out of the house.

Even as Clarissa was being asked for a decision on the limited options on offer from Mr Mulhurst, Michael looked to the window.

He considered it as a means of escape

then immediately dismissed the idea.

What had he been thinking of, asking her — or nearly — to marry him?

A sort of madness had taken hold of him, one which Clarissa had decided to treat almost as a joke, humouring him.

So he imagined.

★ ★ ★

'Sorry about that,' Clarissa said, returning to the living-room. She frowned, puzzled at seeing Michael standing as if poised to leave.

It seemed almost that what had just taken place a few minutes ago had never happened.

'I should be going,' he said lamely.

'Oh? Well, I'm sorry you couldn't stay longer.'

She gave him a candid look.

'Have I said or done something to offend you?'

Michael appeared appalled that his recent behaviour might have made her think that way.

'No, of course not, Clarissa! Absolutely not. I just thought that perhaps I had come at an awkward time, that's all.'

'It's not the time that's awkward,' Clarissa responded.

She shrugged.

'Still, I shan't keep you. You must have better things to do.'

She was hating herself as she said these things and felt it made her sound rather pitiful.

Michael remained where he was.

'You know that that's not true. I came here because I wanted to see you! I still do.'

Clarissa sighed. What was she to say to him? She was in an impossible situation.

She didn't even have any money to spend on herself — her father saw to that.

She felt sorry for having put Michael in this embarrassing position, where he was forced to pretend he wanted to see her.

It made her more annoyed as she considered the fact that he might merely be patronising her, especially after his performance a few minutes ago.

What had that been about?

'I'll see you out.' Her voice was cold.

'Clarissa!' Michael called as she started to leave the sitting-room.

Surprised, she stopped and turned to face him.

He approached, took her in his arms and pressed his lips to hers.

At first there was no response. Clarissa was shocked by this unexpected and passionate attention.

She wondered, again, if Michael was being entirely rational.

But then her own lips responded to his and for a brief time they shared a consuming desire for one another.

It was only the intervention of the telephone — yet again — that separated them.

'I should get that.' There was both reluctance and intimacy in her tone and expression.

Michael let her go.

It was the fishmonger, ringing back to

say he could supply some halibut, after all, for tomorrow.

When she returned, Michael was looking at his watch.

It seemed he really did have to go, but at least he had made his feelings known to her.

And she was glad that he was now aware that she shared those feelings.

She came deeper into the room, but there wasn't the same atmosphere. The spell had been broken.

They looked at each other. Were they both wondering how they could rediscover that magic moment?

'Would you like any more tea?' Clarissa offered with a polite, impartial hostess smile.

'No, thank you. I really should be going.'

He hesitated. Clarissa raised an eyebrow and waited.

'I was wondering about us going to the cinema — or even a meal — or both. I'm on leave till next Monday.

'What do you say?'

'That would be nice,' she replied non-committally.

'What about tomorrow, then?'

Clarissa frowned.

'Could I let you know, Michael? Can I ring you in the morning?'

He looked puzzled but nodded.

'Of course. Fine.'

And on that impersonal, polite note they parted.

Unexpected Phone Call

Clarissa was hovering over the telephone the following morning, wondering whether or not to call Michael and take him up on his offer to go out with him.

She had just decided that she would give him a call when the telephone suddenly rang, making her jump.

Feeling certain it must be Michael she quickly lifted the receiver.

She began talking, convinced it was him on the other end of the line.

In that brief moment she could almost believe a kind of telepathy existed between them.

It was only when a woman's voice interrupted her gabbling that she realised it was nothing of the sort.

'Clarry? Are you OK?'

Only one person had ever called her Clarry.

'Lorrie? Is that you?'

'Yes. Who did you think it was?'

'Oh, no-one,' she answered vaguely.

'It's so nice to hear your voice. How's everything?'

Clarissa was now wondering what her friend was doing phoning her all the way from Germany.

'Oh, all right, I suppose. Can I come and see you?'

Clarissa was astonished.

'See me? Well, yes, but when?'

'Right now, if that's OK with you.'

'Where are you phoning from?'

'I'm at my parents'. I'll be with you in ten minutes.'

And before Clarissa could say anything, Lorraine had hung up.

Something was obviously wrong.

Clarissa had become accustomed to people contacting her only when they had a problem.

She had not heard from her friend in months.

Now, out of the blue, she had come all the way from Germany and was on her way to see her, no doubt with bad news concerning her marriage.

Clarissa moved away from the phone

in the hall, still puzzling, and totally forgetting that she had been about to phone Michael to arrange an outing either the cinema or a restaurant.

★ ★ ★

Clarissa was unaware that Michael was waiting, first of all with hope but then, as time passed, with resignation.

Clearly Clarissa had come to her senses and had decided she didn't want to see him, after all.

It made him feel a fool that he had revealed his feelings to her, something which he decided would not be happening again.

'I'll be going back to Scotland in the morning,' he told his parents later that day as the phone remained silent.

'I thought you still had the weekend before you had to go back,' his mother queried, puzzled and a little upset.

'I'm sorry, Mum, but this Suez business has meant that everyone's leave has been cut.'

Seeing the look of concern on his mother's face, Michael now felt guilty for worrying her.

He went over and gave her a hug.

'It's fine, Mum, I'll be OK.'

But it was clear that his words didn't convince her.

'I've Left Him!'

Clarissa opened the door and stepped aside to let Lorraine in. They gave each other a brief hug in the hall.

'Where's Helen?' Clarissa asked.

'At my parents'. She was asleep so it didn't seem fair to wake her. You'll see her soon enough.'

There was something ominous about that last remark but Clarissa let it go for the time being.

'Come through to the kitchen; I'll put the kettle on,' she invited. 'Then you can tell me what's wrong.'

Lorraine followed her friend and sat down on one of the chairs at the table.

Clarissa, with her back to her, filled the kettle and put it on the gas ring, taking her time to strike a match to light the gas.

She knew she was somehow trying to put off the inevitable. She had recognised the signs in Lorraine's face — not sadness, exactly, more an image of someone not getting their own way and not prepared to compromise.

Clarissa felt defeated even before the conversation started.

'Here you are,' she said, placing a rather utilitarian cup and saucer in front of her.

'Right, you'd better spit it out.'

'I've left Terry,' Lorraine said.

Clarissa rolled her eyes.

'I can see that. Terry's in Germany and you're here.'

'He's not in Germany, he's in Egypt.'

Clarissa's mouth fell open in shock.

'Egypt? And you've left him! How could you, Lorraine? At a time like this!'

Lorraine, stirring her tea, seemed unwilling to look Clarissa in the face.

'There's never a good time,' she muttered. 'I didn't choose it intentionally.'

'Well, it looks like that to me. Does Terry even know?'

'Oh, he knows, all right!' Lorraine was recovering her spirit. 'It's been on the cards for some time. He doesn't understand that I want to be more than just a mother and a soldier's wife.'

Clarissa had to stop herself from saying, 'I told you so.'

But what else could she tell her friend? It was no use her coming all this way hoping for sympathy and some pearls of wisdom that would make everything right again.

That wasn't going to happen.

'It's a pity you didn't think of all this before getting involved with my brother. Who, if you remember, was engaged to someone else at the time.'

Lorraine looked angry. No doubt this wasn't what she'd come here to be told.

She could have stayed at her parents to be told such home truths.

'I shouldn't have come.' She stood up. 'It was a mistake; you're obviously going to take Terry's side.'

Clarissa sighed.

'It's not a question about taking sides. You've got a child to consider; it's no longer all about you. Sit down!'

She spoke so firmly that Lorraine sat back down obediently on the chair.

'What is this all about, Lorrie?' Clarissa spoke in a soothing tone. 'Have you fallen out of love with Terry?'

Lorraine shrugged, then shook her head.

'No, it's not that.' She sighed. 'It's because I do love him; that's why I've left.'

Clarissa frowned.

'I don't understand.'

'You wouldn't. How could you? You've never been in love. It can be the best thing and the worst thing.'

Clarissa tried to swallow her hurt pride.

'Perhaps you ought to tell me, then. Tell me how awful it must be to be married to someone who loves you and with whom you have a beautiful baby!'

Lorraine looked ashamed.

'I'm sorry, Clarry, that came out wrong. But don't you see? Terry is putting all our happiness at risk all over this stupid Suez nonsense.'

'It's hardly Terry's decision, is it? He's a soldier and he has to obey orders. You knew that when you married him.

'I understand you being worried, but there's nothing you can do except support him. Leaving him won't help!'

Lorraine said nothing but was obviously taking in all that her friend had been saying.

Clarissa stood up and refilled the kettle.

'You're right,' a contrite voice said behind her.

She turned, to see her friend wiping away a tear or two from her eyes. Immediately, Clarissa came and put her arms around her.

'Don't cry, Lorrie. I didn't mean to be harsh. I just know you two are meant to be.

'I understand it must be hard for you and I don't suppose, when Terry signed up, he was expecting this.

'But he'll need you all the more now with this Suez stuff going on. You do see that, don't you?'

Lorraine nodded her head vigorously, like a child. It made Clarissa realise how young and inexperienced her friend was.

'Come on, wipe away those tears and let's work out a plan. Has Terry actually left yet for Egypt?'

'No, not yet.'

'Right, so let's get a telegraph sent to his barracks. Maybe he'll get a chance to phone you and you can reassure him that you will be going back.'

'Can't I stay with you for a while, Clarry?'

She obviously saw the puzzlement on Clarissa's face and hastily continued.

'I don't mean actually stay here; just spend time with you before I go back.'

'Won't you want to go back and make things right with Terry?'

'I will. I do. It's just I've missed seeing you and doing things together like we always used to.'

Clarissa looked closely at her friend. She seemed to imagine that by running away you were running back to the life you used to have.

But everything had changed; not only for Lorraine but for herself as well.

'I know, I miss it, too. But we have to adjust to what is happening now.'

'I don't like what's happening now!' was Lorraine's petulant response.

'Neither do I, Lorrie. But you must see, surely, that you're only making matters worse by coming here? I'm sure Terry must be missing Helen as much as he's missing you.'

'I'm not so sure about that, Clarry. It's so much a man's world, the Army. We're just wives.

'I never thought I was terribly important, but being an Army wife makes you feel as if you don't count at all.'

'I'm sure Terry doesn't see it that way. He loves you.'

'Does he? Or does he just love the Army? I'm a sort of accessory as far as he's concerned.'

Clarissa suspected that whatever she might say to be positive, Lorraine would turn into a negative. But only hearing her friend's side of the argument did not give Clarissa a balanced picture of what was going on.

She was about to speak again when the phone rang.

'I'll have to get this. I won't be long.'

She hurried into the hall, half hoping it would be Michael telephoning to say how much he wanted to go out with her.

'Hello?'

'Sis? It's me, Terry. Is Lorraine with you?'

'Terry!' Clarissa immediately lowered her voice to little more than a whisper. 'Yes, she is. What on earth is going on?'

Mystery Woman

For some time after Lorraine had gone, Clarissa sat at the kitchen table. The cup of coffee was rapidly cooling as her mind was on so many other things.

Why, she was wondering, did people create problems when there was no need.

She compared her own life with that of her friend and Terry's and wondered what they had to complain about.

It was not that she felt hugely aggrieved with how her life had, so far, turned out. But when she compared hers to Terry and Lorraine's she could not understand why they felt so unhappy.

Then there was Michael, who no doubt saw Clarissa as stuck in a permanent rut.

She viewed them all not with contempt, exactly, but anger. That they could only see what they didn't have, not all those things going for them.

Michael didn't escape this anger, which she put up as a defence mechanism against the risk of being hurt. Of loving him without there ever being any realistic chance of him returning her feelings.

All right, so they'd kissed. But wasn't that the way with some men? Look at her brother, kissing both his fiancée and Lorraine. It didn't mean much to him, clearly.

At least for the time being, things were settled between Terry and Lorraine.

She was going to stay in Chepswell for a week or so. It would give her parents a chance to get to know baby Helen.

As far as Terry knew, his regiment was on standby at present. All leave had been cancelled but, as yet, there was no date set for their departure to the Middle East.

So, actually, it had proved quite a good time for Lorraine to 'leave' her husband.

Clarissa looked at the clock on the wall. Ten past twelve and nothing achieved.

Just more time passed in thinking about other people's problems instead of her own.

'I suppose I haven't got any, really,'

she mused.

On the surface that was possibly true. No-one could know how dissatisfied she was with her present situation.

No-one would be aware of how unloved she felt, both from her father and, in a different way, from Michael.

It was no use dwelling on such things. She stood up, went to the hall and put on her coat and scarf. Gathering up a basket and a shopping list, she left the house.

The bus she caught just along from her house took Clarissa to the central terminus in town. From there one could get a coach or bus to just about anywhere else in southern England.

On the journey into town Clarissa speculated which destination she would opt for, given the chance.

Berkshire? Hertfordshire? Hampshire?

They all had their appeal, Hampshire in particular. Especially the New Forest with its ponies and moorland, forests and streams.

Clarissa closed her eyes, allowing the unexpected sunshine to rest on her face, imagining the peace, quiet and sweet-scented heather.

'Terminus! All change! All change, please!'

The conductor's voice brought Clarissa back down to earth. She stepped off the bus and quickly merged with the crowd. A mass of people all rushed in different directions, like some frenzied whirlpool.

It was as she attempted to make her way out of the bus station that she saw Michael. He was in uniform with a duffel bag slung over his shoulder.

She was almost facing him and at once hid behind a pillar in the covered section of the terminus.

It wasn't that she didn't want to see him; she just didn't want to see him like this.

The young woman who was with him put her arms around his neck and squeezed him as if her life depended on it.

Michael responded with his free arm, holding the young woman closely around her waist.

Clarissa, breathing rapidly, turned her back on this romantic scene, a feeling of desolation encompassing her.

When she turned to look back, both figures were gone. Clarissa made her way out of the terminus, trying her best to put on a brave face for the world.

World? Her world was about four square miles in size!

At least Terry, Lorraine and Michael were seeing more of the planet.

She continued walking in a blank state, trying to understand why Michael should have called on her and showed affection towards her when he obviously had a girlfriend.

Perhaps that was how men were, she considered. Terry had certainly shown he was capable of two-timing, so why not Michael?

Even her father, Clarissa suspected, was seeing someone. The constant going out, the elaborate preparations beforehand, all told a tale.

In her father's case, Clarissa had to admit he was perfectly entitled to see whoever he chose, being a widower.

Yet if that was the case, why all the secrecy?

She had reached a point in the high street where she needed to cross the road.

It was almost clear to the central island but for a coach heading slowly towards her. London Victoria was its destination.

She waited at the kerb, not looking at anything, just waiting for the coach to go by.

As it almost passed her Clarissa looked up, straight into the eyes of Michael who was looking down at her wearing the same surprised expression.

There was no time for anything else; the coach had passed and was now picking up speed.

Going, going, gone.

Clarissa remained at the kerb till the vehicle had disappeared, out of sight and out of her life.

'Let's Have Fun!'

'Say you'll come, Clarry. It'll be fun!'

Clarissa sat opposite her friend in the sitting-room. Baby Helen was sound asleep in her pram a little way off.

Outside, on this early November afternoon, a weak sun was still trying to brighten what had been a dull day.

'I don't think so. And I certainly don't think you should, either. You're a married woman with a baby, for heaven's sake!'

Lorraine took a deep breath.

'Everyone, Clarry, married or not, is entitled to a bit of fun now and then! And that's all I'm after.

'It wouldn't do you any harm to let your hair down for once.'

'What do you mean?'

'I'm sorry for saying this, Clarry, but you always look as if you've got all the worries of the world on your shoulders, and that's not right.

'You need to give yourself a break. All

I'm asking is for you to come with me to the Pav, just for a couple of hours or so. We'll dance together. It'll be like the old days, remember?'

Clarissa did remember. The Pavilion — or Pav, as it was more affectionately known — was the local music and dance venue in Chepswell.

She had often gone there on a Saturday night in the past, mostly with Lorraine and much to her mother's disapproval.

It was, as her friend said, a place to let your hair down. To have a laugh, get yourself chatted up by a nice-looking boy or two, then buying a bag of chips for the bus ride home.

Thinking of those days now made them seem a whole lifetime away, and not just for her, it seemed.

Clarissa looked at her friend, a wife and mother yet not even twenty.

How swiftly the things that changed your life for ever happened, at just the time when you should be pleasing yourself.

'You said yourself how lonely you get,

stuck in here on your own with just the radio for company. It would be something to do for old times' sake.

'Come on, Clarry, be my best friend again and say you'll come.'

Clarissa's eyes narrowed.

'You're going anyway, aren't you? Does Terry know?'

Lorraine suddenly looked sheepish.

'He won't mind,' she said in a tone that suggested she wasn't altogether convinced.

'He wants me to be happy.'

She looked again at Clarissa.

'And I want you to be happy, too. Oh, Clarry, give yourself a break!'

Clarissa was now certain that Lorraine was primarily doing this for her own benefit. It never looked good, a girl going to such a place as the Pav on her own.

Still, she was tempted.

It would be nice to do something for herself for once, something that would take her away from the everyday drudgery of domestic life.

To be free of all responsibility, if only for a few hours, would be wonderful.

'OK,' she said. 'But we mustn't be late back.'

Lorraine leaped from her chair and hugged Clarissa.

'Thank you, thank you! You'll love it, you'll see.'

At the Pav

Saturday night at the Pav was aimed at their younger clientèle. The resident band, Johnny And The Swooners, provided fairly acceptable covers of the popular songs of the period.

If you'd had enough to drink, you wouldn't notice; if you hadn't had enough to drink, you probably should have done.

After they'd placed their coats with the cloakroom girl Lorraine and Clarissa entered the vast ballroom, with its surrounding gallery above where drinks could be bought and consumed at tables.

'Let's get a drink, shall we?' Lorraine suggested enthusiastically.

They took the wide stairs to the gallery.

'I'm buying them,' Lorraine said. 'What's yours?'

'I'll have a Babycham, please!'

They were already having to raise their voices as the music seemed louder up here, resounding off the ceiling.

'There's a table over there, Clarry. You grab it while I get the drinks!'

Clarissa sat down at one of the few spare tables, guarding it from any who dared to approach.

'There you are,' Lorraine said, returning with a Babycham for Clarissa and a dark concoction in a tall glass for herself.

'Thanks. What have you got?'

'Vodka and blackcurrant. It's the 'in' drink right now. Try it.'

Lorraine held the glass to Clarissa's lips, tilting it slightly as she took a tentative sip. All she could actually taste was the blackcurrant.

A moment later, however, the vodka started to kick in.

'What do you think? Good, or what?'

'Mmm, nice. I might have one later.'

'That's the idea, Clarry, live a little. Cheers!'

They clinked glasses together.

Johnny of the Swooners was singing 'Heartbreak Hotel' and, as far as Clarissa was concerned, was making a pretty good job of it.

The combination of the song's lyrics and the small sip of Lorraine's drink seemed to be making her quite emotional. She knocked back her drink and stood up.

'Come on, let's go and dance.' She held out her hand.

Lorraine quickly drained her glass and took Clarissa's hand. They ran together down the stairs and found a space on the dance floor.

Lorraine was the more expert dancer but Clarissa was happy enough to be moving around in a rhythmic way, her whole body relaxing and loosening up as she did.

She felt almost liberated; all her worries, all her disappointments fell from her like autumn leaves in a breeze.

'Life's a breeze!' she shouted to Lorraine, spinning round as she did.

Lorraine laughed, spinning around too.

Johnny And The Swooners finished the number and then went straight into

'Singin' The Blues'.

'This is my all-time favourite!' Lorraine shouted.

'Really? It's so sad!'

'That's how I was feeling when I first heard it.'

'But you're not sad now, are you?'

For answer, Lorraine shook her head and took hold of her friend and got them both dancing in a rocking, waltz style.

A spotlight circling around the crowd above settled on the two girls.

'Look, we're stars!' Lorraine shouted in Clarissa's ears.

She, though, wasn't quite as keen as her friend at being picked out. She was enjoying herself but wasn't one for drawing attention to herself.

'I've got to go to the Ladies,' she said, disengaging herself from Lorraine.

'Righto, I'll get more drinks in.'

They went back up the stairs, parting at the top.

'Same again?'

'No,' Clarissa said. 'I'll have one of those vodka and blackcurrants, please.

But, here, I'm paying.'

She took her purse from her bag and handed Lorraine a 10-shilling note.

'Will that cover it?'

'Yes, that's fine,' Lorraine said.

It would easily pay for them to have doubles!

Some minutes later Clarissa emerged from the Ladies and searched for her friend.

'Over here!' Lorraine called out.

Clarissa could just make her out. She was seated at a table a little further from where they'd first sat.

But she wasn't alone. Seated with her were two youths.

Clarissa made her way, a little apprehensively, towards them.

This wasn't what she had been expecting; what she had hoped for was that she and her friend could enjoy themselves together. Not be out on a manhunt.

Besides, it was taking a liberty, Lorraine patently flirting with men in full view of someone who was not just a lifelong friend, but also her sister-in-law.

Someone who also happened to be aunt to Lorraine's daughter.

It was then that she became aware that Lorraine was no longer wearing her wedding and engagement rings. Surely not intentionally?

'I've got you a drink, love.'

Lorraine held the drink out to Clarissa just as one of the young men quickly stood up and pulled out a chair so that she might sit down.

'Thank you,' Clarissa said but without making eye contact, which meant that the smile on the young man's face was rather wasted.

'What is that?' Clarissa asked Lorraine, eyeing suspiciously the drink which her friend was still proffering.

'Same as before but with more blackcurrant in it for you, seeing as you can't hold your drink.'

Deciding it would seem ungenerous not to accept what her friend had got her (despite the fact that she had actually paid for it) Clarissa grasped the drink.

She took a tentative sip, watched all

the time by the young man who'd pulled her chair out for her.

'Well?' Lorraine demanded.

'Nice. Fruity.'

She took another, longer sip, feeling a warm glow pervade her whole body.

It really was a very nice drink; an 'in' drink, Lorraine had called it.

'By the way,' Lorraine said, 'this is Gerry and that's Christopher.'

She waved her arm in an expansive gesture, leaving Clarissa no wiser as to who was who.

'Would you like to dance?' the young man, who was in fact Christopher, now asked Clarissa.

She hesitated, thinking of Michael, but this person was distracting enough in the looks department to make her reconsider.

After all, she reasoned, she and Michael had never committed themselves to each other.

Apart from that one kiss there was nothing else to show that they were anything other than friends. Not necessarily good friends any more, judging by the way they had last parted.

'OK,' Clarissa told Christopher.

Before standing up she took another, longer sip of her drink. It really was rather nice — fruity and thirst quenching.

Standing up, she experienced a slight dizziness and took hold, somewhat inelegantly, of Christopher's arm.

He put his other arm around her and guided her gently down the stairs and on to the dance floor.

Like Moses parting the waves Christopher, holding Clarissa's hand and leading the way, got them to the middle of the floor where he now turned to face her.

There was a moment's pause as the previous song ended and the next one struck up. Johnny And The Swooners now slowed the tempo as the lights in the ceiling dimmed, and Johnny led in with 'Love Me Tender'.

Christopher gently drew Clarissa towards him and together they slowly swayed to the tune.

'I'm afraid I don't know your name,' Christopher whispered in Clarissa's ear.

'Clarissa. Clarissa Symons. And you are?'

'Christopher Rankin.'

Clarissa nodded dreamily and then tucked her head close into Christopher's shoulder. This was pleasant, she was thinking. She didn't want it to end.

Then the music finished. The lights went up and the compère of the night's show appeared on the stage to hope that everyone had had a good time and to wish them goodnight.

'I must go,' Clarissa said.

She was feeling a bit panicky, as if she had overslept. Where was Lorraine? She was holding the cloakroom tickets.

'What is it?' Christopher asked. 'Have you lost something?'

'I must find Lorraine. She's got our cloakroom tickets.'

'I'll help you. Come on.'

Once again, he took Clarissa's hand. He led her up the staircase, this time at a faster pace than when they had come down.

Lorraine was nowhere to be found. Neither was the boy — Gerry, or whatever his name was.

'I'll try the Ladies,' Clarissa, now almost frantic, said.

Christopher pulled her back.

'They're the first things the management close,' he told her. 'They want to get everyone out as fast as possible.'

'What about your friend? Where's he now?'

Christopher shrugged.

'He's not exactly my friend. And I guess, like your friend, he's gone as well.'

'What will I do? I've got no coat! I can't go home looking like this.'

'I can take you home. I've got a motorbike. You could wear my jacket.'

Clarissa considered the offer doubtfully. But what was the alternative?

She could hardly expect her father to come and get her — she'd rather walk than face his silent disapproval.

But she didn't know this boy and she'd

heard bad things about people who rode motorbikes.

Come to think of it, though, the arguments had come from her mother who, like her father, disapproved of most things which did not conform to convention.

'Thank you,' she finally said. 'I hope it won't take you out of your way.'

Christopher drove carefully and considerately to Clarissa's home.

For her part, she felt glad to be wearing his warm jacket, the smell of leather being, for some reason, both comforting and exciting.

She had even overcome her trepidation about putting her arms around his waist. It was so . . . intimate, somehow.

After a while even that gave her pleasure: the warmth of his body and the nearness of her own adding to a sort of subdued thrill as the journey progressed.

The Ride Home

'I live just here,' Clarissa called out as they approached number 48.

Christopher switched off the engine and allowed the Triumph to coast to a stop.

'Thank you for the lift,' she said as she tried her best to get off the pillion with as much grace and dignity as she could manage, given her slightly tiddly condition.

She saw the lights in the house were out. Father must be in bed. She hoped so.

'Shall I see you — ?'

'No, thank you. Sorry.'

Clarissa thought he was going to ask to see her again. That was something which, in the chill night air and with a headache coming on, she didn't want, despite Christopher's good looks and manners.

'Don't be sorry.' He smiled. 'I just thought you might like me to walk you up to your front door.'

'No, thank you.'

'I hope you enjoyed yourself tonight.'

'Yes, it was fun.'

'Nice house,' Christopher remarked as Clarissa straightened out her dress. 'Have you always lived here?'

Clarissa frowned at the strange question.

'Yes. Why?'

'No reason. Perhaps we might do it again some time. Or go for a meal?'

Clarissa's resolve weakened. Here was this charming, considerate boy asking her out. Where could the harm be in that?

She couldn't be loyal to a memory. Michael was gone, up in the air in Scotland or wherever, living his life. She had no right to expect him to be waiting for her.

'OK. I'd like that.'

'Which one? The dance or the meal?'

A meal sounded an very attractive proposition, after all the food she'd had to prepare since her mother's death.

'A meal would be nice.'

'Any particular evening?'

Clarissa thought about it. Wednesday would probably be best.

That was her father's Masonic night. He'd rejoined his lodge. He always left early and stayed out quite late.

'Wednesday would suit me best.'

'Great.' Christopher's smile broadened. 'I look forward to it. Goodnight.'

He kissed Clarissa on the cheek.

Indoors, with the sound of Christopher's motorbike fading away, Clarissa walked through the unlit hallway and up the stairs.

The house's quiet was such a contrast to the noise and brightness she'd experienced earlier. Despair started to overwhelm her.

This wasn't how she expected her life to be. She'd wanted to be an artist, mixing with like-minded souls, painting in vibrant colours, going to exhibitions.

Yet here she was, tiptoeing up the stairs so as not to disturb her father, whose manner towards her was as oppressively silent as the house they lived in.

* * *

As Christopher steered his motorbike to the gate of Clarissa's home he had noticed a car parked on the drive. It was a very familiar car — his boss's car.

It was a mystery why it should be here, or why Clarissa Simmonds should be claiming it as her home.

It was, in fact, the home of Geoffrey Symons, his boss. Symons as in Sigh-Mons, Geoffrey never having adopted his wife's affected way of pronouncing their surname.

But Clarissa might be telling the truth. After all, she looked suited to be living in this neighbourhood. And she had been quite specific about the directions.

Christopher shrugged, looking again at the car. He knew this was his boss's car because of the personal number plate which matched his initials.

Growing Up

Lorraine called round the following morning with Clarissa's coat. She had collected it last night with her own but then 'couldn't find her'.

She was now using it as armour against her friend's displeasure at Lorraine disappearing without her.

'Sorry about last night,' she said, handing over the coat. 'We somehow got separated. I did look for you.'

'Of course you did.'

Clarissa looked at Lorraine's left hand and saw that her rings were back on her finger.

'Are you going to ask me in?'

Without waiting for an answer, Lorraine walked past Clarissa and into the kitchen.

'I'll put the kettle on, yes?'

Clarissa followed in behind her, to see her friend putting the kettle on to the gas ring.

'You sit down, Clarry, I'll make the tea.'

Clarissa watched her friend busying herself with the tea-making process.

She knew Lorraine was buying time, hoping this gesture would compensate for her behaviour the previous night.

Clarissa also knew they hadn't become 'separated' but she wasn't sure of the reason why. Or, worryingly, what Lorraine had done in those missing hours.

'There you go.' Lorraine put a cup in front of Clarissa then sat down on a chair.

'Did they have your wedding ring in the cloakroom as well?'

Lorraine looked down at her hand.

'What do you mean?'

'You weren't wearing it last night.'

'I didn't want to worry about losing it, that's all.' She took a sip of her tea. 'Anyway, what happened to you? You seemed to be getting on well with whatsisname.'

'Christopher. Yes, he seems nice.'

'Nice? I should say he's more than nice. And he certainly took a shine to you. I saw how you danced together.'

Clarissa smiled. Despite everything,

Lorraine was her best friend and she didn't like it when they were at odds.

'Actually, we're going out for a meal together on Wednesday.'

Lorraine squealed with delight.

'You dark horse! Where are you going?'

'We didn't decide. There's an Italian restaurant in the old town district; I quite fancy that.

'Anyway,' she said, changing the course of the conversation, 'what did happen to you last night? You and that Gerry fellow?'

Lorraine shrugged.

'Nothing, of course. Why would it? I'm a respectable married woman.'

'No-one would have known that last night!'

Lorraine frowned.

'I hope you're not lecturing me, Clarry. You seemed to be enjoying yourself. And that was the plan — that we had some fun for a change.

'Everything's so gloomy at the moment. November's bad enough without all this Suez nonsense to add to it!'

Clarissa was astonished at the way her friend could so easily dismiss what was a dangerous crisis which was putting her brother — Lorraine's husband — in danger.

'Don't you worry about Terry?'

Lorraine sighed.

'Yes, naturally I do. But what good does it do? Why should we both be miserable?

'Besides, he sees it all as an adventure. Men never stop being boys, Clarry. The sooner you realise that, the better.'

Clarissa was aware of a hardness in her friend which never used to be there. She seemed cynical and not a little world weary.

There had been a glimpse of her old sparkle last night, but that was not how life actually was any more, for either of them.

Shortly afterwards Lorraine left.

Clarissa was relieved.

Apart from the fact she had housework to get on with, she needed to put space between herself and Lorraine.

Friends they might be, but Clarissa's relationship with her brother was far more important and she felt as if she was betraying him just by listening to Lorraine.

★ ★ ★

Wednesday was warm and sunny. It seemed a good omen.

Clarissa was looking forward to going out this evening. To sit at a table, with a pleasant, smiling face opposite and having a meal cooked and brought to her table to enjoy, was going to be great!

She quickly got through her domestic tasks and, with time to spare, decided to make the most of the weather and go for a walk. Despite the sunshine a coat was still necessary, but not a scarf.

There was a slight breeze which lifted her hair slightly and played over her face as she made her way along Tennyson Avenue.

All the trees in the road were now bare and, ahead, she could see a couple of corporation workmen clearing up the remaining fallen leaves. Thus they maintained — even in her absence — Clarissa's mother's high standards.

As she thought of her mother she smiled, possibly for the first time since her passing. She realised that all Mrs Symons had wanted was the best for her children.

But in doing so she had taken away that spark of independence and personality that both she and her brother possessed.

She'd been so concerned with what the neighbours thought that it took away any spontaneity in her affections or her actions.

With the passing of time Clarissa's heart had softened to the memory of her mother. She wished there had been more time, for her to see that her daughter, especially, was capable of being someone in her own right.

Clarissa's walk had taken her to the end of Tennyson Avenue and now she was facing, once more, the busy London-to-Windsor road. She stood at the kerb, looking across to the open heathland.

She looked down at her shoes. They were not appropriate for hiking — the heath could be quite boggy in places at this time of year. She decided to remain where she was.

The image of Michael entered her head. She wondered how he was getting on in Scotland, if that was where he still was.

She had trained herself not to miss him; to block out the feeling she had had when in his company; when he'd kissed her. But it was starting to come back.

She could see herself with him, over the road, on the heath, her head on his shoulder, his arm around her.

It gave her a feeling of sadness that she wasn't expecting, like a death had occurred which she might never get over.

But that was ridiculous. Michael was a friend — or had been. And now he had moved on. That happened in life, it was how humanity progressed.

She couldn't imagine that he was

harbouring these feelings that she was experiencing. Although he was not like Terry he was still a man.

Men, it seemed, existed on a different plane to women.

In that moment Clarissa realised that she had transitioned from a girl to a woman, without anyone but herself noticing.

It was also her twentieth birthday, something even she hadn't realised till this moment, along with everyone else.

'Stop it,' she ordered herself.

Just then a lorry came whizzing past. A youth in the passenger seat leaned out of the open window and called out to her.

'Hello, darlin'!'

Smiling, Clarissa turned from the kerb and headed back down Tennyson Avenue.

At the Restaurant

Clarissa had arranged to meet Christopher at the end of Chepswell high street.

Although her father had already left for his meeting she did not feel comfortable allowing Christopher to call at the house.

Was she was beginning to think like her mother? No, actually, she simply didn't want anyone relaying the news to her father that a boy on a motorbike had called for her.

It wasn't worth the grief it might cause.

She got off the bus shortly before seven and Christopher was already waiting for her.

He was no longer wearing the leather outfit designed for riding his motorbike.

This evening, underneath his dark grey overcoat he had on a light blue suit in the Italian style that was popular amongst the younger men.

'Hello, Clarissa. You look lovely.'

He held out his hand to take hers,

which she did. Against the chill of this early November evening his hand felt warm encompassing hers.

'I booked us a table for seven thirty. I thought maybe we could have a quick drink in the Nag's Head. It's only a little way past the restaurant.

'OK with you?'

'That would be nice, thank you.'

Christopher smiled. Clarissa couldn't know he was secretly laughing at her quaintness. But she was also very good looking and worth nurturing till he tired of her.

He took her hand and they walked along the nearly deserted high street in the direction of the Nag's Head.

Clarissa felt happy and safe. Her father's meeting place — the Masonic Hall — was out on the edge of town, so there was no risk of being seen by him.

Nor would any of her late mother's acquaintances be out at this time of day. An evening sojourn for those suburban wives would take place only at weekends.

So she was enjoying this sense of

liberty and independence, of being more like someone of her age.

And it was pleasant to feel her hand in Christopher's.

Just as they were nearing the restaurant he steered her over the road.

'There's the Nag's Head.'

They walked into the saloon bar. It being a weekday there were very few customers in the bar.

'What are you having?' Christopher asked once Clarissa was seated at a small table.

'I'll have a lemonade and lime, please.'

Christopher looked puzzled.

'Really?'

'Yes, thank you. I might have a glass of wine with my meal.'

Christopher shrugged.

'Right you are.' And he walked up to the bar to order.

Clarissa looked around at the décor of this place. She felt a slight shudder go through her as she did.

It was quite chilly in here. The furnishings were rather tatty and the wallpaper was in dire need of being replaced.

A picture of a sailing ship (why?) on one of the walls was so faded that the only colour remaining was a very pale blue.

The landlord, a grizzly, surly-looking man, acknowledged Christopher's presence by a slight lifting of his head.

As Christopher ordered the drinks a voice through in the public bar called across.

'What you doing in the posh bar, Chris? Are you on the pull?'

Christopher frowned and put his finger to his lips. But Clarissa had heard every word and was feeling anxious now instead of happy.

Christopher came over with the drinks.

'There you go,' he said, placing Clarissa's glass in front of her.

He was watching her face, perhaps trying to guess whether she had heard what his friend, Trevor, had just asked.

Better to pretend it never happened.

'Cheers.'

He raised his pint of beer and waited

whilst Clarissa picked up her glass.

'Here's to a happy evening,' he said with enthusiasm.

Clarissa smiled but without warmth. Her mood had switched from one of anticipation to one of apprehension.

Christopher knocked back more than half of his pint with ease, then looked at his watch.

'Couple more minutes,' he said, putting his glass back down on the table for a moment. 'Have you ever eaten Italian food?'

Clarissa nodded.

'Yes. When we went to Italy.'

Christopher's eyes widened.

'You've been abroad? Blimey, I wouldn't mind that. The only chance I had was when National Service came up.

'Luckily for me, I got turned down.'

Clarissa was puzzled by this.

She could see nothing outwardly wrong with Christopher but didn't feel she had the right to ask.

He picked up his glass and knocked

back the rest of his pint in the same fashion as he'd done previously.

Standing up, he offered his hand to Clarissa, but she was in no frame of mind to accept it.

Instead, she made a pretence of looking for something inside her bag.

'Best be moving,' he told her, making impatient gestures with his fingers.

They walked silently and separately towards the restaurant.

Christopher made no attempt to take Clarissa's hand as they crossed the road.

She suddenly saw it as an analogy of her love life. When she'd gone for a walk with Michael he'd taken her hand as they crossed the busy London road.

And if he was here now, she'd let him again.

She no longer had an appetite either for Christopher's company or the food they were about to order.

Before going into the restaurant, they paused outside. There were only a few patrons dining.

As Clarissa's eyes moved amongst the

people they suddenly widened.

Christopher noticed her reaction.

'What is it?' he asked.

His own eyes were screwed up to try and identify what Clarissa had seen.

Whatever it was, it had certainly shocked her.

She turned to face him.

'I'm really sorry,' she said, 'but I've got a really bad headache. I just don't feel hungry. Thank you. Goodbye.'

She swiftly moved away, leaving Christopher bewildered.

He looked again inside the restaurant, then his own heart began beating fast.

It was definitely him! And it was definitely her.

Christopher swore under his breath and looked down the high street. Clarissa was gone.

'Win some, lose some,' he muttered as he made his way back to the Nag's Head and the more convivial company of his mates in the public bar.

* * *

Clarissa, on the bus heading home, was only now starting to gather her thoughts together.

She thought again about what she'd seen when glancing into the restaurant's window.

Despite the low level of lighting, there was no mistaking him.

What had thrown her, however, was the smiling face and animation that her father was displaying towards the woman he was sitting opposite.

Clarissa had no idea who that woman was but, because they were in profile to her, she could see that she was considerably younger than her father.

Clarissa felt sick. She would have got off the bus but there was still some way to go before her road.

A fog was now starting to form in her head. She sat immobile, unable to get the image of her father looking so happy out of her head.

Why could he not have shown some sort of warmth towards her? Ever?

A smile and a kind word could have

made all the difference to Clarissa's dull, enforced life.

What this new sense of her father did was fix in her mind a purpose.

Things were going to change.

A Doppelganger

'How was your Lodge meeting, Father?'

Mr Symons looked up from his boiled egg, a peevish expression as usual on his face.

Clarissa had begun to wonder if it really had been her father she'd seen in the restaurant last night. But she clung to the recollection and to the fact that he had been with a younger woman.

'You know I don't discuss such things, Clarissa. Not with you, not with anyone. Why do you ask?'

'No reason. It's just a most amazing coincidence, that's all.'

Mr Symons was getting visibly irritated.

'What is?'

'Well,' she said, sitting down at the table opposite him, 'I happened to be in the high street yesterday evening when I saw a man in that new Italian restaurant who looked exactly like you.'

Mr Symons had probably chosen the

wrong time to put his cup to his lips, as he choked in response to Clarissa's words.

She continued as if nothing had happened.

'They say, don't they, that everyone has got a doppelganger, so I suppose that's what I saw. Besides, this person was with a young woman.

'And you were at your Masonic meeting, weren't you?'

She stood up and went to the kitchen, not allowing her father to either admit or deny what she had told him. She just wanted him to know that she knew.

She busied herself, waiting for either her father to come out and explain what she had witnessed or for the sound of the front door closing as he left for work.

Neither happened so she nervously returned to the dining-room to clear the remaining breakfast things from the table.

Mr Symons was seated in one of the wing-backed fireside chairs with his newspaper. But he wasn't reading it.

He looked up at his daughter, watching her as she cleared the table.

'Another cup of tea, Father?' Clarissa asked with false brightness.

Her heart was racing uncomfortably underneath the housecoat she always wore at this time of day.

'No, thank you. Come here, Clarissa and sit down. I have something to tell you.'

Michael and Terry

Clarissa had arranged to meet Lorraine in the Littlewoods café in town. Ironically it was the same place that Terry had first encountered Eleanor.

So much water had passed under the bridge since then. Terry was a married father, Clarissa was an aunt and their father, whether he wished to acknowledge it or not, was a grandad.

Clarissa wasn't sure where Lorraine stood. She was the wife of Terry and the mother of their child, yet she behaved as if she was neither of these things.

And now this meeting, arranged over the phone by Lorraine.

Mr Symons hadn't even begun to tell Clarissa whatever it was he had to say to her when the telephone rang.

Whilst Clarissa was answering it her father had slipped out of the house, leaving her questioning what he had to tell her, and if he ever would now.

The moment had passed and Clarissa's

former courage in telling her father what she knew had deserted her.

'Hi, Clarry. Thanks for coming.'

Lorraine sat down opposite her friend, removing her gloves as she did so.

Clarissa saw that her wedding and engagement rings were still there, so some things seemed back to normal.

'I got us a coffee each and a Danish.'

'Yummy!'

After they'd had a bite of their pastries and a sip of their coffees, Lorraine spoke.

'Two things to tell you. First, I'm going back to Germany. I expect you'll be pleased.'

'I am. What changed your mind?'

'Terry. He phoned and told me they'd been stood down and were no longer going out to Egypt.'

'Oh, I am glad! I've been so worried.'

'Me, too. And I have missed him. I just didn't feel he appreciated me or Helen.

'He seemed to prefer the company of his soldier buddies to me.'

'Well, I'm sure that's not the case, but I'm glad you see it, too.'

'Yes. I do love him and, frankly, staying with my parents has been unreal. They've been treating me like a child — as if I'm Helen's sister, not her mother.

'I understand, in a way, but it gets a bit tedious to be told to tidy my room. Me, a married woman!'

'Still, they've been very good to you. And they babysat whenever you wanted to go out. Which reminds me, what did happen between you and that Gerry fellow when you took off without me at the Pav?'

'Nothing, I told you. He did try it on, but that's when it hit home that I shouldn't be doing this.

'My main reason for going to the Pav was to take you out of yourself; to remind you that you're young and ought to be able to enjoy yourself once in a while.

'I know we're in the same boat, but all I do is for the benefit of my husband and daughter, not my ungrateful old father.'

Clarissa decided to let that remark pass.

'You said there were two things you

wanted to tell me. What was the other?'

Lorraine took another bite.

'All this Suez business meant that there were a number of combined forces sent over to Germany to be in position for when the whole silly nonsense kicked off. That involved the RAF as well as the Army.'

'And?'

'And there was a concert organised so that all the servicemen could meet up. That was where Terry met Michael Parkes. He's in the RAF, doing his National Service.'

'I know.'

Lorraine leaned forward.

'Anyway, your Michael —'

'He's not my Michael,' Clarissa argued, but Lorraine continued with her news.

'Well, he and your brother got into a bit of an argument.'

'What?' Now it was Clarissa's turn to lean forward. 'What on earth could they have been arguing about.'

'You!' Lorraine announced almost triumphantly.

'Me?'

Clarissa was astonished. Why would anyone squabble over her? What on earth did either of them say?

There they were, in military uniform, with all sorts of dangerous issues taking place in the world, getting into a heated exchange over her!

She could not imagine the situation Lorraine was describing.

'Yes,' Lorraine continued, 'you. And it was Michael who started it.

'Things had begun amicably enough, but once the two of them recognised each other I'm afraid Terry made some sort of jokey remark about Michael hanging around his sister.

'That seemed to set Michael off. He reminded Terry how often he'd let you take on a lot of his problems — and mine, obviously. He said it was so unfair that you had been left to look after your dad while Terry was doing exactly what he wanted.'

Clarissa didn't know what to say to this at first. She had no idea how strong

Michael's feelings were towards her.

Then that little, undermining voice in her head suggested that it was because he pitied her, not loved her.

'What happened next? Did they actually start scrapping?'

The term scrapping, she realised as she said it, didn't seem as serious as fighting. Boys scrapped and it meant nothing.

Men fought and it was deadly serious.

'They would have done but various people intervened and separated them. I must say I was a bit ashamed of Terry. He had no right to have a dig at Michael.

'After all, he's a friend of yours, so why would Terry make such remarks?'

Clarissa shook her head.

'I don't know. Like you say, Michael and I are friends; nothing more.'

Clarissa felt a desperate need to get away, to be by herself. Suddenly so many things were going on that, in different ways, were having a profound effect on her life.

There was still that business with her father who, for once, actually wanted to tell her something.

And then this, with Michael, willing to get into a fight over stupid things her brother had said about him and her.

She wondered what evidence Terry had had, to say things like that. It never occurred to her that her brother might be trying, in some strange way, to be protective of his sister.

Or that he might even be a little jealous of her. His life was all mapped out — Lorraine and the Army had seen to that. Mostly he didn't seem to mind. But perhaps there was a part of him that missed the freedom he'd once had.

'I have to go, Lorrie. Thanks for telling me.' She stood up to leave.

'We'll see each other before I go back? You'll want to say goodbye to your niece, won't you?'

'Of course I will. Ring me when you know when you're returning. Bye.'

She turned and left before Lorraine had even a chance of standing up and kissing her goodbye.

The high street was busier now.

Clarissa checked her watch — it was midday already. People were starting to come out to lunch from all the various offices and factories hereabouts.

She hadn't gone far when a figure stepped in front of her. Without looking, she went to move past, but again the figure blocked her way.

Clarissa looked up into the eyes of Christopher. He was smiling at her as if everything in life was a huge joke.

Clarissa was glad she had realised that he had merely seen her as a trophy, something to crow about with his mates.

'Hi, how are you? Sorry you had to rush off yesterday. Are you OK now?'

'Yes, thank you. I just didn't have the appetite for a meal. I'm sorry.'

'Yes, it was a shame. Something seemed to spook you when you looked in the restaurant. Was it my boss?'

'Your boss?' Clarissa was confused.

'Yeah, the old guy sitting with the young girl. I didn't notice myself till later, when he and his secretary came out of the restaurant as I was passing.

'I must say,' he added, 'he was very surprised when I said hello to them both. You should have seen the looks on their faces!'

Clarissa, although she was well aware of the hour, looked at her watch.

'Oh, dear, is that the time? Sorry, I must go. Nice talking to you.'

She broke into a run to get away from him as quickly as possible.

He called out to her but she wasn't listening. She'd heard enough.

Shocking News

From the kitchen, where she was preparing the evening meal, Clarissa heard the front door open. Her heart began beating rapidly.

'Deep breaths,' she told herself.

By doing this she was able to control her emotion sufficiently just as her father entered the hall.

She stepped into the hall to greet him.

'Good evening, Father.'

'Clarissa,' he replied, always his form of greeting to his daughter. A cursory acknowledgement of her existence.

He walked past her and into the sitting-room where he sat in one of the armchairs and lit a pipe.

Clarissa's stomach was in a mass of knots.

Now or never, she decided as she walked into the sitting-room.

Mr Symons glanced up, taken aback by her unexpected presence.

'Father, I need to speak to you.'

Mr Symons folded up his newspaper and laid it on the arm of his chair.

'I'm sure you do,' he said quietly.

Surprised and a little encouraged by his words and tone, Clarissa began.

'Who were you with on Wednesday evening? You know, when you said you were going to the Masons.'

Mr Symons slowly turned his head to look directly at his daughter. Clarissa faced him out; after all, she had nothing to lose.

'Because I know you didn't go. I know because I saw you in that Italian restaurant, having a meal with a woman.'

There, it was said. What was the worst that could happen now? Despite trying to reassure herself, her heart continued to beat rapidly and her head was pounding.

Instead of getting up out of his chair and shouting at her, Mr Symons remained seated, his head now turned away from his daughter.

There was a long moment of silence.

'Come here, Clarissa,' her father said,

quietly and in a tone that did not suggest anger or irritation. 'Sit down. I need to tell you something.'

Clarissa stepped towards the other armchair and sat down on the edge of it, as if she might suddenly have to take flight.

Mr Symons tapped out his pipe in the ashtray and left it there, the residue of tobacco sending up little plumes of smoke as it burned itself out.

Clarissa found herself focusing on that rather than look directly at her father.

'I am thinking of getting married again.'

Clarissa felt she must have misheard. Her father remarrying?

'This is rather sudden, isn't it?' was all she could find to say.

'Well, no, actually. I have worked with Valerie — Miss Buckley — for a number of years and we seem to get on well enough.'

He said this in an almost light-hearted fashion, as if there was nothing unusual about it.

Clarissa felt there was more to this than her father was telling.

'So that was the woman I saw you with in the restaurant? Miss Buckley?'

Mr Symons nodded.

'Yes, it was.'

'Were you ever going to tell me that you were going to get married, or would I have learned of it in the local 'Gazette'?'

Clarissa's indignation was giving her courage, something her father must be beginning to be aware of. It was now his turn to be nervous.

'It's not as easy as that. Nothing's been decided, not definitely. I have to consider all aspects of what it might mean.'

'I don't understand. Are you marrying this Miss Buckley or not?'

'I will be, yes. It's just she doesn't want to live here — or anywhere in Chepswell, come to that. Her family is from Cardiff and she wants us to move there.'

Clarissa was bewildered.

'What about me? Where do I fit into all this?'

'You could always move there with us,'

Mr Symons offered, but there did not seem to be any enthusiasm in his offer.

'How could I? I won't know anyone there. And you'd expect me to move into a house with a complete stranger!'

Mr Symons looked at his daughter with an aggravated and puzzled look.

'This is my home, here,' Clarissa persisted.

A terrible thought came to her.

'What if I don't want to come? Where will I live?'

Mr Symons climbed out of his chair.

'We're nowhere near that stage. Who knows where any of us will be tomorrow?'

His expression suggested that this discussion was over. He walked past her and out of the room.

★ ★ ★

That night Clarissa couldn't sleep. The news her father had told her kept going round in her head without any resolution.

What made it worse was that she had no-one to share any of it with.

Lorraine was too busy with her own affairs. Besides, this time tomorrow she would be back with Terry in Germany.

As for Terry, she loved her brother but for him other people's problems were just that — other people's problems.

She had been surprised to hear from Lorraine how he and Michael had almost come to blows over her, but that, now, was irrelevant.

At the thought of Michael she felt an aching in her heart. It hurt, making her sob quietly into her pillow.

Was there no end to this misery that she was experiencing? If only Michael was here now she would tell him what she was feeling.

That she loved him; would always love him and wanted to spend the rest of her life with him.

'Silly girl,' that niggling little voice in her head said. 'You only want him as a means of getting yourself out of this predicament.

'You had your chance — chances! Why didn't you tell him then? He told you enough times.'

And in this muddled, miserable frame of mind Clarissa drifted off into sleep.

Uncertain Future

The morning following life-changing news tends to put things in most people's lives into perspective.

For a brief moment, after waking, Clarissa felt as she always did at the start of a new day. Resigned.

But soon the remembrance of the previous evening's events returned to haunt her and, instead of getting up, she lay back on the pillow, intending to remain in bed till she heard the front door close behind her father as he headed off for work.

She drifted back off to sleep and thought she must be dreaming when his voice called up the stairs.

'Bye, Clarissa. See you this evening.'

The front door shut before she had a chance to respond.

She continued lying there, aware of the silence that often pervaded the rooms of this house.

She tried to remember the last time

she'd heard anyone laugh here. It could only have been Lorraine, perhaps. She often saw the funny things in life, even when they weren't.

Clarissa allowed herself to think more about her friend. Her upbringing hadn't been so different from her own, yet she seemed to have made more of her life than Clarissa had done.

Maybe that wasn't altogether true. Did someone really want to be married and with a child, and not yet twenty-one?

Right now, the idea was not an unattractive one. There was love and laughter in Lorraine's life.

Even her parents were making the best of it — they doted on their granddaughter and were going to miss her terribly when Lorraine took her back to Germany.

But it was hard to imagine her father holding any such feelings of affection towards Clarissa or any child she might have. He was so wrapped up in his own little world.

It had not been that obvious when

Clarissa's mother was alive. She had always held sway over the house and its running.

Her death had left a huge void, not so much in people's lives but in the house itself. The house represented status and standing in the community and those who inhabited it had to abide by and maintain its upper-middle-class values.

Clarissa wondered how she would even begin to cope somewhere else. And where would that somewhere be?

She could not for one minute imagine herself in Cardiff, living in a house shared by her father and his new wife.

But what would be the alternative?

Suddenly she saw a positive aspect of this situation. She could get a job and find herself a bedsit or whatever young, single people lived in when they'd left home.

Then her optimism faded. That seemed more lonely and bleak than her present situation. At least, in theory, she was in charge of this house; every room was her domain.

There was the expansive garden as well. That was one thing in all this that she had really come to enjoy. Gardening afforded her creative, even artistic, freedom.

From growing flowers to display, to vegetables and salads to eat, she had expressed, in part, some of her creative talent.

There would be none of that if she lived in a bedsit. She'd be like a bird in a cage where the outside world was only visible behind bars.

Deciding that these thoughts were doing her no good, Clarissa threw back the sheet and eiderdown and swung her legs over the edge of the bed.

Stepping across to the window she drew back the curtains and was surprised to see sunshine bathing the garden in a warm glow. A surprising end to November.

There was a month to Christmas. The thought filled her with a sort of dread.

In her mother's day it had been something to look forward to, but since then it had offered neither comfort or solace.

She, obviously, would have to buy her father some sort of present. Last year it had been a tie which she'd never seen him wear.

If only Terry, Lorraine and little Helen could come, but that was very unlikely. Her brother had used up most of his leave prior to the Suez crisis.

It made Clarissa feel almost desperate to find a way out of all this, for herself. But she recognised that her situation was, as it had always been, dependent on others — namely her father.

It was like a riddle that just couldn't be solved.

She washed, dressed and was downstairs just as the telephone rang.

'Chepswell two, two, three,' Clarissa said, unwittingly sounding as businesslike and formal as her mother had done.

'Clarissa? Clarissa, is that you?'

It was a very poor line.

'Hello, hello! Who's calling? Who is this?'

'It's Michael, Michael Parkes.'

Clarissa was both shocked and pleased at hearing Michael's faint voice.

'Are you there?'

'Yes, Michael, I'm here. How are you?'

'I'm fine. It was a surprise to see you at the bus terminal that day!

'Aileen had come to wave me off, but it would have meant a lot to say goodbye to you before I left for Scotland.'

Aileen? It had been his sister she'd seen him with, then!

'I have news which I wanted to share with you.

Although she was pleased that Michael wanted to share whatever his news was with her, Clarissa was surprised that he would.

They had not spoken in ages and she hadn't been encouraging when they had met.

'Go on, then.'

The line faltered, crackled and then cut Michael off completely.

He tried twice more but without getting more than a couple of words out.

'Write to me!' Clarissa shouted.
But the line was silent yet again.

Michael's Letter

With Christmas almost here Clarissa made some attempts at making the house look festive. She bought a wreath for the door with money she'd put by over a number of weeks.

Every bit of loose change she'd got back when shopping was earmarked for the procession of carol singers who always targeted Tennyson Avenue, expecting such an affluent area to be rich pickings.

Often they would be disappointed and would find more generosity existing in the smaller working-class homes of Chepswell.

She left the purchase of a tree to her father but he, instead, dug up the one he'd bought last year which had, surprisingly survived and in fact had grown a little in the intervening twelve months.

It was planted in a pot and placed on the occasional table in the sitting-room.

All it needed now was the baubles, tinsel and cotton-wool balls to complete its transformation. But every day Clarissa put it off. It was as if it would make a farce out of the whole business.

Christmas in this house would be a joyless affair, as it had been ever since Mrs Symons had passed. There was no sign that this year was going to be any different.

Then, out of the blue, just a week before the big day, Clarissa's father delivered a bombshell.

'There will be one more for dinner on Christmas Day,' he told her, taking a number of pound notes from his wallet. 'This ought to cover the cost.'

He passed the money across to Clarissa, who didn't immediately take it.

'Who's coming?' she wanted to know, while knowing full well who he had in mind.

'Miss Buckley, the lady I told you about.'

'Ah, yes. The lady you're going to marry and move to Cardiff with. I know.

'Am I to call her Miss Buckley when she's here or would you prefer me to call her 'Mother'?'

Mr Symons looked flushed and angry.

'There is no need for that, Clarissa. You can call her Valerie.'

He turned to go, leaving the money on the sideboard.

'I hope you will make her feel welcome.'

Clarissa had no words to respond to that. Even when she disliked someone she was never rude.

The post brought its usual dross plus a few Christmas cards from far-flung relations that no-one even remembered.

Yet they would receive the same warm greeting as they themselves had sent.

We simply must meet up this year.

Amongst all the seasonal fare was a letter, addressed to her and with a Scottish postmark.

Michael!

Clarissa gathered up all the post and went through to the kitchen. Putting aside the cards and bills, she sat down at the table and carefully opened the letter.

Dear Clarissa,

I'm sorry I couldn't get through the other day, it was a very bad line. I hope you are well. I expect you're busy making preparations for Christmas.

What I wanted to tell you is that my National Service has come to an end and that I will be staying on in Scotland, having been offered a job as chef at Glengarth Castle's restaurant, which is near to where we have been based.

I'll tell you all about it when I see you which, I hope, won't be long as I'm coming to my parents for Christmas before heading back north to take up my new appointment.

I shall be at Chepswell from December 22 to 31. I hope very much you will see me, as I have something important I want to say to you — something which I have already mentioned to my parents.

Unless I hear differently I'll telephone before I call on you.

Love, Michael.

Clarissa was baffled by Michael's letter. What was he trying to say? That he wanted to bid her goodbye before setting off on his exciting new venture?

And what could there be that would require him to discuss it with his parents?

It was strange and left her feeling disturbed and, to some degree, disappointed.

'Well, maybe I won't be in when he calls!' she told herself, but her voice lacked conviction.

Curiosity, if nothing else, drove her need to know what he meant by the things he said.

Besides, her heart wanted to see him, to be near him, if only for one last time.

Despite everything, Clarissa continued with preparations for Christmas at home with the extra guest, Miss Valerie Buckley.

Maybe she would be all right, Clarissa considered, although she still couldn't imagine what this woman could possibly see in her father.

Then she remembered his smiling, animated face in the restaurant. Perhaps he had finally found the love of his life.

There had never been much to indicate that he and Mrs Symons held any passionate feelings towards each other.

The most Clarissa had seen was her mother taking his arm when out walking on a Sunday afternoon, or the peck on the cheek he gave her before setting off for work.

Yet, there must have been something that had brought them together; some sort of attraction. After all, here she and Terry both were, evidence of their parents' feelings.

Time and familiarity seemed to have dried up whatever passion they might have had, like an arid desert.

She put Michael's letter in her bedroom cabinet and tried to put it out of her mind. She had things to be getting on with.

She was nervous about meeting Valerie Buckley. How would she react?

In some ways it would be a relief that someone else was about to take away the responsibility of looking after her father.

Clarissa had found it a thankless task and would be more than happy to pass it on to someone — anyone — willing to please him!

What Love Means

It was a couple of days later, on the 20th, that Clarissa, having fought her way through the crowds in Chepswell high street, returned home with a banging headache and sore feet.

She couldn't understand why they called Christmas the season of goodwill — she'd been elbowed, shoved, had both feet trodden on and been given some hostile looks from other shoppers.

She couldn't wait for it all to be over, not least because she could not imagine how Christmas this year would turn out in her own house.

She made her way to the sanctuary of the kitchen, found the box of matches and lit the gas under the kettle. Then she collapsed into the chair as she waited for it to boil.

She recalled, in a sentimental way, the Christmases of her childhood — well, hers and Terry's.

They had been good, exciting, with all

the magic associated with a child's vision of that special time. Of Santa on his way in his sleigh, led by Rudolph and all the other reindeer.

Of carol singing, of snow gently falling and settling as they sang those much-loved, familiar tunes.

Even when the magic faded as the children grew older, Christmas still remained that one special time of year.

It was as if Clarissa's parents had had a spell cast over them, making them more affectionate and more indulgent than they normally would be.

But ever since Mrs Symons's untimely death no such spontaneous joy had come into the house. Clarissa felt the hypocrisy involved with decorating a tree and putting up paper chains and suchlike.

Even the hoped-for festive weather seemed to have disappeared. There was no snow forecast over the Christmas period — in fact, the weather had turned unusually warm for the time of year. December 22 came and with it a feeling of nervous expectation on Clarissa's part.

She tried to remind herself that, just because Michael had written that he would be arriving on this date, it did not follow he would suddenly turn up on her doorstep.

There would be his parents to consider; unpacking and catching up with news.

That was why, just after one o'clock, the sound of the doorknocker almost made Clarissa jump out of her skin.

'Michael! How nice to see you. Come in, come in.'

She was so busy gesturing him inside, her arms going like windmills, that Michael could not have got close to her to kiss her even if he had wanted to.

It was possible, subconsciously, that that was what Clarissa was doing — fending him off because she didn't want to be hurt or disappointed by what Michael had come here to say.

'In the sitting-room.'

She pointed, but Michael stopped walking.

'I'd rather go into the kitchen, if that's OK. It seems less formal.'

Clarissa wasn't sure what to make of this request. It was true that the kitchen was more cosy and relaxing than the sitting room. It was also warmer.

'Right you are, follow me.'

She was still trying for a light-hearted manner, which was in complete contrast to how she was actually feeling.

She needed to be strong for what he was going to tell her. Bad news travelled fast, she remembered. Michael couldn't have got here much quicker if he'd flown to her house!

'Tea or coffee?' Clarissa offered as she put the kettle on to boil.

Michael, instead of sitting at the table, came round to where she stood by the oven, having lit the gas under the kettle.

'Clarissa, can we talk?'

He looked so determined, in a gentle way, that she put the kettle down and turned to face him.

'What is it you want to say?'

He took both her hands in his. She didn't resist, but neither did she respond. She felt she knew what was coming.

Just get it over with, she was praying.

'Clarissa, I can't be sure what your feelings are for me, but I expect you know how I feel about you.'

'It's all right, Michael. You don't have to say. I understand.'

Michael looked both surprised and pleased at this revelation.

'Do you? Well, then, all the more reason that I tell you.'

He drew her closer to him. Clarissa half turned her face away from him. The expression 'cruel to be kind' ran through her head.

'I love you, Clarissa. I love you with all my heart. I've never felt this way about anyone else.

'As soon as I saw you at the fair that time I knew you were the one. I just hope you feel the same way about me.

'Look at me, Clarissa. Please.'

Very slowly she turned to face the handsome face before her. She felt an emotion which was part sadness, part hopelessness.

'I'm sorry, Michael. Truly I am.'

* * *

Michael frowned and then an awful truth dawned on him. All during the time he'd spent shilly-shallying around his feelings for Clarissa, she had gone off and found someone else.

He let go her hands. What had he been thinking of? Of course she'd met someone else!

Why wouldn't she? She was a beautiful young woman; she had a presence that he found mesmerising, but in truth she was out of his league.

'No, I'm sorry. I shouldn't have come. I should have realised you would have met someone else.'

'Someone else?' Clarissa interrupted. 'I haven't met anyone else.'

'Then what? Why? You just don't love me, is that it?'

She sighed in frustration.

'It's not as simple as that. My feelings don't come into it, really.

'I'm not sure what love is, you see. And what I've seen of it hasn't impressed me,

I'm afraid.'

Michael saw, through this bleak narrative, a glimmer of hope.

'Clarissa, I want to show you what real love means. It means putting the person you care most about before anything and anyone else. It's sharing all life's ups and downs together.

'Put simply, it's like being one and the same person. And I do truly love you. I would never hurt you or let you think less of yourself.

'My only purpose would be to make you happy; to bring a smile to your face. Please, Clarissa, give me a chance.'

Suddenly she put her arms round Michael's neck and kissed him. He returned that kiss with equal passion.

'Oh, Michael,' she whispered as their lips briefly parted. 'I do love you.'

The kettle started to whistle. Michael reluctantly released his hold on Clarissa.

'Tea or coffee?' she asked, her voice shaking.

Michael opted for coffee.

'Then I would like you to listen to what I have to tell you, my darling.'

A Scottish Adventure

It was more than an hour later that Michael finally set off back to his parents' house.

In some ways Clarissa was glad to be on her own. It would give her time to take in all that he had said.

The news about his job was amazing. Now he was out of National Service he had landed a top position at the castle close by his RAF base.

Although he'd told her that in his letter, he'd failed to add that there was a cottage to go with the job, and also how it had all so fortunately come about.

He and other members of his crew had made the restaurant and bar their local, as it were. On one particular evening the resident chef had phoned in sick, causing all manner of problems for the owners, Mr and Mrs McVie.

'It was a bit like when someone in a theatre calls out to ask if there is a doctor in the house!' Michael told her.

'Anyway, I stepped forward and offered my services.'

'How did that go down?'

'Really well. I just love being in a busy kitchen, serving up meals. I felt so completely at home.

'I'd already fallen in love with Scotland, especially this area of Drumlochan. You'd love it, Clarissa, I know you would. It's an artist's paradise.'

Clarissa was pleased that Michael was acknowledging her artistic talent; it showed how much he thought of her as a person in her own right.

He went on to tell her how the McVies had been so impressed they told him if ever he was looking for a job there was one there for him at their restaurant.

'Apparently their present chef hadn't really taken to Scotland and often made excuses not to come to work.'

'So you'll be off to Scotland. When are you going?'

'They want me up there for Hogmanay. And I've agreed.'

'That's great,' Clarissa said, but

without really feeling it.

'Well, it will be, if . . .'

And that was when Michael asked Clarissa to go with him, to be his wife and live in Scotland in the cottage he was being offered.

At first she didn't know what to say. On the surface it seemed like a dream come true.

But it was just a dream, she was certain. How could she leave?

Now Clarissa had had a little time to give it more thought, she couldn't see any reason not to go.

She loved Michael and he loved her. He was offering her happiness, something she'd not known for a very long time.

There was just one thing getting in the way of her agreeing to his proposal.

Her father.

Michael couldn't understand her.

'Surely he wouldn't try to stop you?'

She shook her head.

'It's not that, Michael. I just don't see why I should have to ask his permission to get married.'

Michael's eyes lit up.

'Well, then, let's elope!'

'Elope?'

'Yes.' He took Clarissa's hands. 'We can do that in Scotland.

'We can go to Gretna Green and get married. Then you wouldn't need your father's permission. Oh, Clarissa, it's perfect!'

She laughed shakily.

'What about your parents? Wouldn't they mind?'

'Not at all. They've never been ones for occasions of any sort. And I think they might find the journey too much for them.

'Besides, there isn't time to do it any other way. I'm supposed to be starting my new job on the 31st.

'So, Clarissa, what's it to be? Will you come or not?'

And that was how she had left it, without making a decision.

She didn't want Michael to believe that she had any doubts about her love for him. It was just the timing. Christmas.

She would have to stay at least for Christmas Day itself; it wouldn't be right to spoil things for her father and Valerie by sneaking off.

No, she would stay and have Christmas dinner with them and then make arrangements with Michael to travel up to Scotland to marry.

The plan was both reckless and exciting, a total contrast to the sort of life she'd only ever known.

Clarissa went over to the phone in the hall, picked up the receiver and began to dial Michael's number.

Whole New World

The long avenue of trees they were passing between was not as long as in Tennyson Avenue, but was impressive nevertheless.

The beeches, bare of any leaves, stretched their long branches right over either side. In summer it would make this approach more a tunnel than an avenue.

Clarissa was more thrilled, excited and happy than she'd been in her entire life.

She snuggled up against Michael in the back of the chauffeur-driven Daimler which had been sent to collect them from the small station at Drumlochan.

This was the last leg of their epic journey which, two days previously, had taken them from Chepswell up to the Scottish Borders where a taxi had driven them the final few miles to the blacksmith's at Gretna Green.

After the wedding Michael had booked them in to a bed and breakfast close by. In the bedroom Clarissa had put pen to paper and written a second letter to her father.

She had already left a note in the sitting-room, telling him that she had left and that she would explain shortly where and why.

Christmas Day had not been as bad as Clarissa had expected, something almost certainly due to the presence of Valerie Buckley.

Clarissa had wanted not to like her but could find no reason to do so. It still puzzled her, though, as to what attracted Valerie to her father. Only time would tell.

The trouble was, Clarissa's sense of duty and consideration for others had almost got in the way of the plans she and Michael had made for the start of their life together.

She had begun to feel guilty, a feeling compounded by Valerie's own consideration for her.

Still, perhaps that would make it easier for any reconciliation between daughter and parent when the time — hopefully — came.

Clarissa had not kept her forthcoming marriage a secret from her brother and Lorraine. Although they couldn't attend, of course, they had sent a congratulatory telegram.

Michael's parents and his sister had also made a contribution, paying for their overnight stay and the rail fares for both of them.

'Happy?' Michael was looking down at his beloved bride.

'Very,' she responded in a contented tone.

Her head contained nobody's problems; her thoughts were just immersed in her own pleasure and the anticipation of a better life.

They passed through the avenue of trees, coming out of it and into this whole new world that was opening up before them.

We do hope that you have enjoyed reading this large print book.

Did you know that all of our titles are available for purchase?

We publish a wide range of high quality large print books including:
**Romances, Mysteries, Classics
General Fiction
Non Fiction and Westerns**

Special interest titles available in large print are:
**The Little Oxford Dictionary
Music Book, Song Book
Hymn Book, Service Book**

Also available from us courtesy of Oxford University Press:
**Young Readers' Dictionary
(large print edition)
Young Readers' Thesaurus
(large print edition)**

For further information or a free brochure, please contact us at:
**Ulverscroft Large Print Books Ltd.,
The Green, Bradgate Road, Anstey,
Leicester, LE7 7FU, England.
Tel:** (00 44) **0116 236 4325**
Fax: (00 44) **0116 234 0205**

Other titles in the Linford Romance Library:

LORD WINTERTON'S SECRET

Kitty-Lydia Dye

Virtue Browne was once childhood friends with the mysterious Lord Winterton. But now villagers avoid the crumbling wreck of his manor house on the dunes, and gossips whisper that the young lord is involved in arcane rituals. A headstrong governess too inquisitive for her own good, Virtue will encounter romance, mystery and smugglers at her first posting. Is there a logical explanation for the strange things she sees? Or will she become another soul lost in the rumoured secret tunnels?